STEADY NOW

The author, writing under the pseudonym general practitioner. His medical practice has been successfully combined with writing and broadcasting. In total he has written about 20 books, but this is his first novel.

A Yorkshireman by birth, now living in Oxfordshire, he is married with three grown-up children, one stepson and four grandchildren. His first wife, Pam, died seven years ago.

His first broadcast was in 1961, and he has either been broadcasting on Radio and TV or writing books, short stories and articles ever since. He is a well-known after-dinner speaker.

BY THE SAME AUTHOR:
(Warner Books, Little, Brown & Co.)

Just Here, Doctor
Not There, Doctor
What next, Doctor?
Oh Dear, Doctor!
Look Out, Doctor!
Surely Not, Doctor!
There You Are, Doctor
On Holiday Again Doctor?
You're Still a Doctor, Doctor
Three Times a Day, Doctor?
Only When I Laugh, Doctor
It's a Long Story, Doctor
An Arrow Full of Quivers

Front cover illustration by kind permission of
The Yorkshire Ridings Magazine

STEADY NOW DOCTOR

Dr Robert Clifford

ARTHUR H. STOCKWELL LTD
Ilfracombe, North Devon

Copyright © Dr Robert Clifford, 2001
First published in Great Britain, in hardback, 2001
This edition published in Great Britain, 2002

The moral right of the author has been asserted.

All rights reserved.
No part of this publication may be reproduced, stored in
a retrieval system, or transmitted, in any form or by any
means, without the prior permission in writing of the
publisher, nor be otherwise circulated in any form of binding
or cover other than that in which it is published and without
a similar condition including this condition being imposed on the
subsequent purchaser.

All characters and situations portrayed in this book are
imaginary. Any resemblance to persons living or dead is
purely coincidental.

British Library Cataloguing in Publication Data.
A catalogue record for this book is available from the British Library.

ISBN 0 7223 3488-5

Printed in England by Arthur H. Stockwell Ltd., Ilfracombe, Devon.

CONTENTS

CHAPTER 1	From Nonentity to Deity	1
CHAPTER 2	Stage Struck	17
CHAPTER 3	Disaster	29
CHAPTER 4	Dr Andrew Howard	35
CHAPTER 5	Into the Workhouse	46
CHAPTER 6	A Dip into the Well of Pleasure	52
CHAPTER 7	On the Treadmill	64
CHAPTER 8	Fully Engaged	73
CHAPTER 9	The Gods Shone	83
CHAPTER 10	Wedding Bells	93
CHAPTER 11	One of Each	105

CHAPTER 1

FROM NONENTITY TO DEITY

Doctor Andrew Howard lost his virginity at the age of twenty-four, in the third month of his first resident house job to the best looking female Senior Surgical Registrar that there had probably ever been.

She was so good-looking that in her presence even the most eminent surgeons behaved like adolescent schoolboys, and in addition she had an aura of sexuality which made even the hospital Chaplain break into a sweat.

That he should lose his virginity at such a time, would have been a terrible shock, not only to all his friends but also to many of his most brief acquaintances.

One of two things that helped him in his earlier days, was the fact that since the age of thirteen through a misunderstanding at the men's hairdressers, he had always carried a packet of French letters in his wallet. A packet had fallen off the shelf, he picked it up and the hairdresser said, "That will be nine pence."

Recently he had come across a couple of discarded wallets, each still showing the tell-tale ring that French letters eventually engrave through the substance of the leather.

Where today, you might have a supplier of crack or cocaine, in his circle he was the man to come to if you thought you had a chance of having it away. He never charged for his protective sheaths, even sometimes having to steal from his mother's handbag to make sure that he always had a supply of the readies. He would even give the most profound advice on how to go about things. He was thought to be the complete man of the world; even the football captain was in awe of him. What is more, he was completely discreet. No one knew about his conquests, whereas others did it or nearly did it, just to talk about it. Not divulging his secrets only increased his stock.

It would have been greeted with utter disbelief had it became known that it was not until he was 24 that he was literally led by the hand to his first experience of the *Well of Pleasure*.

Andy had no idea whether his birth was planned or not. His sister Lettice (the second support of his early days) was an accident and was one of the reasons for his parents unhappy marriage.

He did not know whether it was being called Lettice (Lettuce is full of the anti-sterility Vitamin, Vitamin E) or his parents unhappy marriage, but, from the age of fifteen there was always a welcome in his sister's body for any presentable interested male. Initially for a bag of sweets, then as the years progressed, a few drinks, to a formal meal until finally at the age of nineteen, it would have to be at least a weekend away with a bit of jewellery thrown in.

She was five years older than Andy, and the only time in his life he was really popular was this period, when boys, men? who were always eight to ten years older wanted to meet his sister, or borrow a French letter or both. She was a lovely girl, and he thought it was a great surprise to her to find that she was carrying around something so precious that all men were after it.

She was a great Big Sister to him making up for his parents deficiencies who were so busy continually rowing that they did not have much time to take any notice of either of them.

Unfortunately, at the age of twenty-one, she got religion, and immediately became nasty. At twenty-three she married a one-eyed Baptist minister and became a typical "mother Grundy" eventually going off with her one-eyed partner to be missionaries in New Guinea.

They never heard from them again and thought that they had probably been eaten by their flock. Although the family never heard from them directly, they did know of people who had, but they never saw them again.

Andy was born in the year of the General Strike in 1926 and felt that this was a significant factor in his life, that he had entered the world on a day when nothing was happening and no one was working.

He went to a variety of schools, the first of which he could hardly remember was a Church infant school, which could have been the reason why many years later the missionaries nearly signed him up. One clear recollection of this school was the open fire with a guard, on which the lady teacher, who seemed to have a perpetual cold, spread out snot soaked handkerchiefs to dry.

He then went to a prep school where he had a dim recollection of doing well, or at least not doing so badly that he was out of step with everyone. Matters were put to rights at his third school which was coeducational. He hated it. It had no redeeming features. Even girls were an additional source of humiliation.

What absolutely terrified him was the swimming on Saturday mornings in the school baths.

He would try and sprain his ankle, have a cold, anything, so as not to have to face the compulsory jump into the baths. Fortunately his father was always on the move to new jobs, and although it seemed a lifetime, he can't have been at the school for more than two years. In spite of these unhappy two years, it was during them that life really began for him.

It all started when there was a knock on the door and a policeman in full uniform greeted his mother with the words, "I have come to see your son about house breaking".

It was the beginning of some of the stormiest weeks of his life. For one short period of time his parents were so busy having a go at him, there was no time to row amongst themselves. He was not sure if that is what they mean when they say children bind a marriage together.

What had happened, was that one day he was walking across the land of an unpleasant farmer, who used to spread the contents of his cess pit either side of the right of way to deter people from straying off the path.

He was with two older boys from his street who had discovered that not only had the farmer moved, leaving an empty farmhouse, but had also left a full basket of eggs in the front room.

The eggs were taken outside and all three boys systematically threw them at the house, covering it with yolk, and for good measure threw a few stones at the windows, shattering a few panes of glass.

One of his more sophisticated companions (they were 11, he was 9), had noticed some games had been left in a cupboard, so he returned that night to purloin them, professionally slipped the catch, then climbed over the window-sill into the arms of a waiting policeman.

His mother had a field day. He would be sent to prison and expelled from school, bringing everlasting disgrace to the family. He remembered about two months after the incident that he made the mistake of coming home from school smiling. How could he smile, et cetera.

The crux of the case was that one police sergeant wanted to take them to juvenile court, and the other sergeant didn't.

In view of their tender years, they were to be spared court if he was prepared to join the Wolf Cubs and the other two the Scouts. This of course he did, and thus began some of the happiest years of his life. He was in his element. Two years later, after another move to another place, he became a Boy Scout and really, now approaching the end of his life, looking back, he realized that he had been a Boy Scout all his life.

As a Boy Scout he won the war against Germany single handed by collecting waste paper in a trek cart, which also gave him the bonus of reading all the personal mail of the beautiful Betty Jameson — always unobtainable, who lived at the top of the road. Many years later when he was a medical student and she a radiographer, he still adored her, and she was always nice to him in a sort of head-patting way, only consorting with men who were at least 10 years older than him.

Another failure.

In 1942 he cycled to his grandmother's house in Blackpool with a boy called Joneson, accompanied for the first day and a half by a boy called Ward. When he and Joneson bumped into each other in later years they wondered why they went together. They weren't even really friendly before or after the immediate event. But in later years they did see each other from time to time, and had joint outings with their wives.

Over the years Joneson became very successful, and was almost running the Common Market at one time. His home in Bath was the most beautiful house Andy had ever been in and in 1992 on the 50th anniversary of their trip, Andy and his wife Mary were invited to a most sophisticated lunch. This was followed by coffee and liqueurs in the pavilion of Bath stone the Jonesons had built on the hill, at the top of their garden for listening to his recordings of Schubert.

It was breathtaking with a wide panoramic view of Bath stretching away beneath them.

Never close friends, but always with a great regard for one another and always wondering what happened to Ward, where did he go, and who he actually was.

Driving back from the Jonesons, for no definable reason, Andy recalled not one of his successes, but what for him was one of the most abject failures of his early years. He could have only been six or seven. The family were staying at uncle Arthur's (with a waxed moustache) and auntie Alice's at Ramsgate. There was a buzz one evening as the next day Lobby Ludd was to be in Ramsgate, and some lucky person who had to be holding a *News Chronicle* would challenge him with the words, "You are Lobby Ludd, I claim the *News Chronicle* prize" — to be awarded £5, which was a fortune in those days. Andy knew it would be he who would win, just as nowadays everybody knows that it will be they who is going to win the Lottery. He intercepted the paper boy and sped off into town clutching the *News Chronicle* — challenging left and right. He spent the day unsuccessfully scouring the town, as his mother, father, aunt and uncle scoured the town looking for this lost little boy, eventually seeking the aid of the Police who found him fast asleep in a deck chair still clutching his *News Chronicle*.

All he won that day was a smacked bottom. He never forgot the incident, the name Lobby Ludd somehow became imprinted in his mind.

* * *

Riding to Blackpool was recognized as a great feat in 1942, never mind Dunkirk, and the Middle East — the boys were 15 years old, cooked their food over wood fires before blackout time, and each had a knife, which as well as blades, had a spike for getting stones out of horses hooves. Joneson still had his diary he made of the event, with entries such as — Ward making a dash for Burton-on-Trent today — and on the finance page, lunch 6d., and 3d. for a tart, later. It must have been an edible one, surely.

* * *

When he was aged eleven, the family moved to Surrey where he attended the local grammar school. He didn't enjoy his days there, but it was from this very school that he met Joneson, and four years later they went off on their great adventure.

He was an indifferent scholar, and was almost always at the bottom of the class — out of 29 he was usually 27th or 28th.

When in his early 40s, whilst clearing out some drawers, he discovered a bundle of reports which only contained one good remark.

The remark, which many a time he had pondered over, sprang out almost in neon lights, in the rows of poors, very poor and does not try. It said, *GOOD WORK IN WARSHIP WEEK*. Now what on earth could he have done to gain acclaim in this week, and what was *WARSHIP WEEK* anyway. His only possible reference was Joneson, and he had no idea.

He was once asked, during a TV interview regarding a new book, "Tell me, Doctor, what were your school days like?"

Nodding wisely, he replied, "It was reported that I was very good in *WARSHIP WEEK*."

The interviewer was momentarily nonplussed. It would be a loss of face to confess ignorance of such an event, so he quickly replied, "That's marvellous, absolutely marvellous," and quickly changed the subject.

In a way this was gratifying for Andy as it is said that everything you do in life at some time serves a useful purpose, and until that TV interview he had not been able to fit *WARSHIP WEEK* into the scheme of things.

He did, at the age of 12, briefly achieve some transitory fame at this school. It was in the end of term boxing, which he hated. He was boxing somebody who was just as bad at it as he was, and they were hurting each other almost to the point of tears, when he noticed, after one right-handed punch, that his hand hurt. When he returned to his corner at the end of the round he told the Games Master, who proceeded to wiggle his hand around, but pronounced it OK. He was not discomforted during the next two interminable rounds, where they almost pummelled each other to death, collapsing in each others arms.

This was an indication of fine sportsmanship, and brought a standing ovation from watching parents and friends. What the crowd didn't realize was that the boys were so shagged out, this was the only way they could stay on their feet.

It should, of course, have been a draw. They were both as bad as one another, but Andy was declared the winner on points.

When they took his gloves off in the corner it was noticed that one of his knuckles was bruised. The St John Ambulance man in attendance was called over for a consultation. He ordered an immediate course of action, and proceeded to put Andy's arm in a triangular bandage, although he didn't feel that there was anything wrong at all. Of course, with his arm in a sling Andy got another round of applause as he left the hall.

His parents were summoned (they had not come to watch him), and they drove to the local hospital where they had to wait two hours for an X-ray. Eventually, a disgruntled Radiographer (he kept on repeating that he had been dragged away from a darts match) held up a negative and said, "He has a hairline fracture of the knuckle of his fifth finger, and will need to keep his arm in a sling for a week".

Andy was delighted by this. It kept him out of doing all sorts of things, including writing.

Word got out that Howard, in spite of breaking a bone in his right hand in the first round, had fought on and won his bout.

Just be careful with him, he doesn't look it, but he's as tough as hell.

Even his parents, who hadn't seen the bout, wondered if they had bred a tiger after all.

But, of course, it didn't last. He was scared of the vicar who taught scripture, so did not put up his hand to be excused, wet his trousers, burst into tears, and from then on he was treated with the usual derision.

It is strange, there was only one other boy from that school that he remembered, apart, of course, from Joneson and Ward, who neither could recall, and that was a boy called Dinga Powell, who he also didn't remember, but his name was inextricably locked in his mind. Dinga Powell's father was a bus conductor, hence the prefix. It was not in any way, as far as he remembered, derisory — he was just called Dinga Powell. When he reminisced with Joneson about Ward he always asked him if he remembered Dinga Powell and he never did. Of course, Joneson was much brighter than Andy, they were never quite in the same form. Joneson was always in 2a, 3a, 4a, 5a and Andy was always in 2c, 3c, 4c, and when it came to the fifth form he wasn't even in 5c, being put in an ambiguous form called remove, but it was from the remove that he had his one triumph — he was good in *WARSHIP WEEK*.

* * *

The trip to Blackpool was some undertaking. When he said our trip to Blackpool, Andy was going to his grandmother, who lived on the South Shore end, and Joneson was going to an aunt, who lived in Lytham St Annes. On reflection, perhaps the subtlety of place of destination was the real difference between them.

Andy and Joneson did all the planning. They thought that Ward joined them for one night only, and Joneson's diary record of, "Ward making a dash for Burton-on-Trent today," confirms this.

They knew he came ill-equipped, as on their first night, where for some reason they pitched their tent on a rubbish dump, Ward had no sleeping bag, and had to share the large hessian one with Andy.

Today this could have all sorts of connotations, but in those days it didn't. That's how things were.

In spite of it being wartime, they had managed to get a route map from the AA. These maps were joined at the top of the page, and had detailed instructions like, turn left at Brown's Tea Shop, right at Smith's Garage, and as you turn up and over each page, the road for you to follow, with all its accompanying details, ran down the middle of the page.

Andy was later than all his friends in acquiring a bicycle. His father was some sort of Structural Engineer, being moved on and up the scale every few years but never quite catching up to the salary scale he was on, so the family was always hard up.

At the beginning of the war the family were evacuated to his grandmother's at Blackpool, but after some months things were so quiet they returned to their home in South London. The day of their return coincided with the first day of the Battle of Britain, and they had a ringside seat watching spitfires and hurricanes fighting against overwhelming numbers of German aircraft over Croydon Airport.

But, joy of joys, some stranded New Zealanders, who had been borrowing the house, had left a bicycle behind. Andy immediately claimed it. It was a sit up and beg bicycle, and had no handgrips on the handlebars. This was remedied by his father, always a genius with plastic wood, who moulded some on. In fact, he was probably the only cyclist with plastic wood handlegrips.

Joneson's bicycle was of the dropped handle, racing type, which had the disadvantage that when he became so tired he couldn't lift his head, which was often, he couldn't see where he was going, so Andy, in his upright position, directed operations.

He was not wearing his Boy Scout uniform as he was not on Boy Scout business, but he did wear his Scout trousers which were dark blue, a leather zipped jacket, Scout socks, plus green tabs on his garters to show that he actually belonged to the Scouts.

He had a borrowed frame rucksack which he wore. His tent, sleeping bag and hand axe were carried on the carrier on the back of his bicycle.

On his belt he had a sheath knife with a silver top, beneath which were two circles of coloured glass between the top and the hardwood handle.

His multibladed penknife hung from a ring on the other side of his belt.

Joneson had some sort of lightweight waterproof gear, and all-in-all looked much more streamlined than Andy.

They went up the old Watling Street that Roman Legionnaires must have marched up in their thousands, and who would have envied their bicycles, as they, in their turn, envied the cars and lorries that passed them.

Nowadays it is not easy to pick out the Watling Street on modern maps with all the new motorways that have sprung up, but he still had a feeling that somehow they went through Grantham, as in one ambiguous town they parked their bikes against a grocer's window, to have the daughter of the house, a bushy blonde with prominent teeth of about their age, come out and hysterically admonish them.

They were a bit nonplussed at the violence of her attack. Fortunately Joneson kept his cool.

"You've got a big hole in your stocking," said Joneson.

"No, I haven't," said the girl, carefully examining her black woollen cladding.

"Yes, you have," said Joneson.

"I'd like to see where," said the girl, now looking worried.

By now they had safe hold of their bicycles.

"Where you put your legs in," shouted Joneson as they cycled away.

One day, many years later, when Joneson and Andy had one of their periodical bump-ins on the train from Paddington, Joneson said, "You remember that blonde at the grocers?"

"Yes," said Andy.

"I bet it was Maggie Thatcher."

"My God, I bet you're right," said Andy, "but only if the Watling Street goes through Grantham."

He remembered Lichfield, Atherstone, Newcastle-under-Lyme, then Warrington to Preston, all cobbles, and he believed it was near Preston he said goodbye to Joneson and, in fact, it was some years before they met again, as he changed schools the next term.

The journey took them four days, and he was given a heroes welcome in Blackpool. His mother and father were there, both pleased to see him. His father more than his mother, not that either liked him more than the other, but if anything had gone wrong with his trip his mother would have blamed it on his father.

His bum was the sorest it had ever been, and he was just about muscle-bound. He was taken to a slipper bath in Blackpool Central the next morning. A slipper bath was just an ordinary bath, one of many in a public bath building. Organizing a bath at short notice at home was much more difficult in those days. For the next few days he basked in the glory of his achievement, then some event of national importance took away everybody's attention.

* * *

His mother and father rowed incessantly. There was nothing so small it could not lead to a heated argument. Several Christmas dinners were spoilt by arguments on how the turkey should be carved, with everybody finishing in tears, and as a finale, his mother locking herself in the coal place.

There are many types of sin. Too many to enumerate. But in his limited experience he felt that nagging was by far the most serious. His mother was an expert. If it had featured as an event in the Olympics, she would have won a gold medal.

An example of her skills was the day his father won some award. She was included in the celebrations, but, of course, not the main event as he was. He was up on the stage, blushing about the nice things that were said about him, received his award to thunderous applause, returned to his seat next to his wife, who whispered in his ear, "Did you know that your suit was shabby?"

Now that was really a class act. She hadn't broken any laws, and perhaps had told the truth, yet in those few quiet words she felled him with one stroke, as surely as one can fell a sapling with an axe.

His father held his own through sarcasm. They were really like two plants in adjacent pots, his father growing more quickly in his than Andy's mother, who tried to keep him down to her size by hacking at his roots.

There must have been times when they communicated. There was rarely a noise from their bedroom, and perhaps this was where they communicated best. It was always a wonder to him how Lettice had been conceived. He learned in later years that it was behind a bush in the dark in some northern park. Surely they couldn't have been arguing then.

His father was a bit of a lad, which was confirmed once when Andy was leading the Peewit Patrol through some local forest. They came to a clearing, and there was his father in his parked car with his secretary. For some reason he didn't seem as pleased to see Andy as Andy was to see him.

That night, when he got home, his father was waiting behind the kitchen door, springing out when he arrived, shoving a half crown into his hand and saying, "Don't tell your mother you saw me."

"What's going on," said his mother with her antennae raised.

"I'm just seeing he's all right," said his father.

Andy couldn't understand any of it. It seemed quite natural to him that his father should take his secretary for a spin, though, for some reason some of his patrol sniggered. Years later his father told him that some of the parents of his patrol cut him dead after this event, but this was probably just his guilty conscience.

This was just about the time Andy was beginning to get religion and thought no evil. His Bible was Baden-Powell's Handbook for Scouts, which clearly outlined what was good and what was bad. Under the heading masturbation it said, "Don't do anything you wouldn't want your sister to know about".

Now there was a time before Lettice got religion, when she would have been quite interested and probably would have encouraged him, but once she had linked up with her one-eyed love there's no doubt she would have been on Baden-Powell's side.

For Andy, who thought he had found something unique that only he knew about, was now in a position where he always meant to stop doing it but of course never did, but from then on had a guilty conscience every time he did it.

Returning to the parental battle, some aspects of it were a complete enigma to him.

In 1938 at the age of 37 his mother decided that she wanted to be an actress and went off for a year to Drama School in Croydon.

Even today this would be a bit unusual. In those days it was quite incredible, and the fact that his parents must at some stage have had a rational discussion to agree it, was almost unbelievable. Sadly, it was eventually to lead to tragedy.

For a year he was a latch-key schoolboy, living off school dinners, which weren't bad, and having unlimited bread and jam as soon as he got home.

He did not get religion as badly as Lettice, but he got it badly enough. When he was fifteenish he joined the Crusaders which was religion for Secondary School children only.

There were camps (nothing like Scout camps) where older men took you for walks and asked you if you had found the Lord. There were Bible meetings, Prayer meetings and on a Sunday Andy went to five different services. He was the complete little prick. He was called by a fellow Christian to come to his sister who was weeping uncontrollably after being jilted by some long-standing boyfriend. Andy knew just what to do. He put his arm round her and said, "Why not turn to the Lord, He succoureth all in need." Hardly turning, she smacked him right in the eye.

He was even elected to, and gave a sermon in church. But he

was getting all muddled up with masturbation, the Scouts, and his parents; so one day in Church he prayed that God would guide him in the Vicar's sermon as to what to do.

He got a surprisingly direct reply.

The Vicar got up into the pulpit and quoted a verse from St Matthew, "Go ye then before all nations baptising them in my name," and he went on to talk about the need for medical missionaries in China.

He had been called.

That afternoon, he went to Crusaders almost in a state of trance. On hearing the circumstances of his calling everybody fell about praying. This went on for weeks.

A man from the China Inland mission called to see him and said that if he did follow his calling the Mission would help with his fees in Medical School.

It was settled; he was going to be a Missionary Doctor. Then one day a boy who had been in the same form at the Grammar School was killed whilst riding his bicycle. He couldn't remember who it was as the only people he remembered from that school were Joneson, Ward and Dinga Powell, and he couldn't remember Ward or Dinga Powell.

The death necessitated a special Crusader Prayer Meeting where they all prayed and wept and also rejoiced, as three days before he was knocked off his bike, whoever it was had accepted the Lord and had been saved.

Suddenly it all didn't seem to make sense to Andy. If he was saved, why did the Lord let him get knocked off his bicycle?

From then on he slowly drifted away from the Church. He couldn't have one logic for everyday life and one for religion.

His departure was slow and he changed from wanting to be a Missionary Doctor to just wanting to be an ordinary Doctor.

As far as he could remember, both through his Baden-Powell and religious days, he was still a supplier of French letters. He always wanted everyone to think well of him. He was also a bit parsimonious in his deliveries during these two phases, accompanying his distribution with smug phrases like, "I'm only giving you this to save some young girl from an unwanted pregnancy."

He never tried, "The Lord succoureth" bit as most of his

recipients were bigger than him.

He continued being a supplier until gradually people had the nerve and the money to buy their own from the chemists or hairdressers, so from then on he experienced a huge fall in status.

When he had definitely decided to be a Doctor his parents sprang one of their surprises.

Somehow in the Remove at the Grammar School he had managed with two other boys to pass the School Certificate, but not well enough to take the Higher Certificate.

His parents, always short of money but who had come up with funds to start his mother's acting career, now sorted out a place for him as a day-boy at a prestigious medical public school.

This was the term after the holiday when Joneson and he had ridden to Blackpool, and was the reason they didn't meet for many years.

The strange thing was that although he had been a nonentity at the Grammar School, because his background and origin were working class, somehow at the public school he became very important. It came about like this.

He had never played Rugby before, but in his second year he received his first XV colours which meant he was almost a deity, and a small boy was even designated to clean his boots. He was made a House Prefect, which meant he could button up his jacket or leave it unbuttoned or something. His success at the public school led the Headmaster to confer with the Headmaster of the grammar school on how the change of social circumstances had affected him, was this some new formula they had stumbled on?

Of course the whole thing was a complete lot of balls. He was just the old inadequate he had always been, but there was a change of circumstances that distorted the picture.

On his first games afternoon at the public school, he was clad self-consciously in brand new Rugby kit, surrounded by groups who had been playing since about the age of three when they went to pre-prep school, then prep school and now public school. Whatever were they going to do with this grammar school oik.

At this school they played games in Houses, and this afternoon they were trying to sort out the House Rugby XV for the School House Rugby Cup Competition. "I know," said one heavily

Brylcreemed six-footer, "we will make him the opposition hooker."

"What's a hooker?" Andy asked. Everybody collapsed with laughter at his ignorance.

"Well," said Brylcreem, "it means you play in the middle of the scrum, and when the ball is put in you have to hook it back on your side."

They patiently had a few practice scrums to show him his duties, then a game was started in earnest. He kept away from all the rough stuff but kept near enough to the ball to take his place in the scrum down when they occurred. He had never played rugger but he had played that despicable game soccer, and was quite good with the ball at his feet, thus whichever side put the ball into the scrum, whether his side were pushing forward or being pushed back, he always managed dexterously to flick the ball back to his side. They tried every combination but he always got the ball.

Reluctantly they had to put him in the House First team and he continued with his prowess to the extent that they were the first dayboy house ever to win the house Rugby cup.

He was moved up rapidly to the school 2nd XV, then the school 1st XV, and was the first player in the school ever to receive both their 2nd XV and 1st XV colours on the same day. Somebody who had his 1st XV Rugby colours at a public school is an outstanding success, even if he is thick as a plank. So he wasn't a triumph of some new planting, he was just good at hooking a rugger ball out of a mound of straining players.

In those days hookers were just hookers, and did not have to know much about Rugby. Nowadays, hookers are expected to rush about with a ball and do all sorts of things.

His hooking stood him in good stead and was as useful to him in his medical school days as providing French letters had been in earlier days. The medical school he went to was Rugby mad. If you were good at Rugby you got a place in the school; if you were very good at Rugby you got a scholarship, so they always had a very good team.

He hooked against Cardiff at Cardiff Arms Park, Swansea at St Helens, and Harlequins at Twickenham and Waterloo in Liverpool.

He met his own Waterloo in the Middlesex seven-a-side competition at Twickenham. He had always kept away from the rougher side of the game just standing around rucks trying to look useful and never ever handling the ball.

In the Middlesex seven-a-side he actually scored a try in the quarter finals against the Harlequins. The other 13 players were all struggling in a heap, the ball squirted out to his feet, he picked it up, took one step forward, placed it down for a try and they had won the game.

In the semi-finals against the London Irish in that vast stadium with only 14 players on the pitch, suddenly for some unknown reason, he was passed the ball. He caught it, stood there not knowing what to do with it, and 25,000 people laughed at him.

He philosophized, anything anyone has never lasts for ever, you just have to use what you've got whilst you've got it. Sadly he was not even able to say that he used to be a good hooker, as the ladies of the streets had pinched the word and like every other area in his life he had explored, the end result was a failure.

He often pondered in quiet moments about those developing years and, one particular Friday evening when in general practice, having been up all Thursday night and worked solidly through the Friday, he looked into the waiting room to see 40 people eagerly waiting his evening surgery. 95% of them wanted only to pour out their troubles, expecting a transfusion of his energy in return. He went back into his room and looked up and in his tiredness thought he saw clouds as opposed to the ceiling, and a kindly smiling face saying, "You see, you didn't get away after all."

CHAPTER 2

STAGE STRUCK

He found, as expected, that getting a place in St Jane's Hospital was not difficult. He had a short interview with an elderly man who coupled his work as Dean at the medical school, with shooting round the world as a physician in attendance to the Prime Minister.

The elderly man looked up from his desk.

"What school are you from?"

"Metson College," he replied.

"Got your Higher Cert?"

"Yes, Sir."

"First 15 Colours?"

"Yes, Sir."

"Did you play for the County or England Schoolboys?"

"No, Sir."

"Right start in October, but keep training during the summer."

There was a pause as the old man seemed to lose interest in the whole interview. Andy shuffled his feet uncertainly.

"Excuse me, Sir," he said, "is there any opportunity of being considered for a scholarship?"

"No," said the old man circling on his chair to fiddle with some papers behind his desk, signifying that the interview was finally over.

Andy sat moodily in the compartment of the train on the way home, his mother would not be at all pleased that he hadn't even the chance of a scholarship.

Arriving home she saw him trying to slip up to his room from the back door.

"Did you get accepted by St Jane's?"

"Yes, Mum," he said trying to look cheerful. "It looks a

tremendous place." In fact he hadn't looked at the place where he was to spend the next six years. He was late for his appointment, ran all the way from the tube, spoke to the Hall Porter, who showed him to a row of seats, three of which were occupied by terrified acne covered Welsh boys who were almost clinging to each other on their first visit from the Valleys to the big city. In fact he could hardly remember anything about the place at all.

"Did you ask about a scholarship?"

"Yes, Mum," said Andy trying to sound casual. "No chance I'm afraid, I was lucky to get a place at all."

It was like walking into a hailstorm. "If you'd only worked a bit harder instead of playing Rugby all the time, all the money your father and I spent on you..." and so on. He just had to stand there and let the words hit him in waves. There was no possible way he could tell her that if he had spent more time playing Rugby, he would have had a better chance of a scholarship.

His mother had now started to cry in her frustration. There was no warmth about her that he could reach and just hold for a bit and sadly indeed her tears were not for him but for herself. She had hoped to tell her drama group, which was getting progressively more important, and taking up more time, that she had a brilliant son. He was only saved by his father, who had seemed to appear from nowhere, but there was so much noise going on that he could have come in through the door in a bren-gun carrier.

"Just shut up, Elsie," he said, "they can hear all this down the street."

"What d'you mean, shut up," screamed his mother. "This lazy lout has let us down." As she turned to his father, he took the opportunity to slip up to his room, he could leave the battle flowing to and fro downstairs. He wondered if all boys who got a place at a medical school went through this.

He lay on the bed nursing his triumph that he'd got past the dragon and could savour the fact that he was now a real medical student.

He began to visualize himself in all sorts of situations: medical officer to an expedition up the Amazon; brain surgeon, no, perhaps discovering a drug like penicillin, perhaps being famous by going out to Albert Schweitzer's leper colony, but underneath it all was an awful dread that he had got a place in the medical school just because he could hook a ball out of a scrum. What if he couldn't pass his exams, having just scraped through Higher Cert? His day-dreaming was interrupted by his mother shouting up the stairs.

"Are you coming down for supper? everything is getting cold."

Suddenly, some sort of energy seemed to flow into him and for the first time in his life he stood up, opened the door, and shouted out at the top of his voice, "No I am not."

His mother was momentarily stunned, then regaining her composure, "Of all the ungrateful louts, all the money, all the sacrifices..." then the flow of conversation eased as the dining room door shut and silence, and they started to eat. He turned, and wearily buried his head in his pillow. He felt as if he had committed a crime, and for no reason at all, he began to weep. He must have drifted off to sleep. He vaguely heard the bus stopping to pick up his mother for an army concert, then he awoke as his door opened. In came his father with a plate of sandwiches in one hand and an envelope in the other. "Where shall I put these, doctor?" he aid.

"Well done lad, a medical student at last and here's something for the holidays. We're all proud of you. Don't be too upset about your mum, she's playing the lead tonight in the play. It's her first time, and she's a but on edge. I've got to go back to the office for a bit, here take this," and threw him the envelope.

Andy ate his sandwiches hungrily, trying to guess what was in the envelope, was it ten shillings or a pound? He wiped his fingers after his last sandwich, and held the envelope up to the light. He began to flood with disappointment as he opened it. No pound or ten shilling note. His father had strange ideas about gifts. He would often leave a raffle ticket as a tip in a restaurant, and if he was giving something away that he no longer had use for, it suddenly became one of the most valuable possessions he had. Andy pulled out a piece of folded white paper and opened it to see what was inside. There was nothing inside but the paper, incredulously nearly as big as a handkerchief, with black writing on one side. *A whole five pound note*.

He had hardly ever seen one, never mind touch one. He turned back to his pillow again and wept. It had been a long day.

* * *

Andy slept soundly, keeping one ear open for the postman's early knock. He had been waiting for this knock with lessening hope for some days now.

There was a knock at about 8 a.m. He was down the stairs before the letter hit the mat. There were six in all, four for his father, who had left for work at 7 a.m., one in spidery handwriting probably from grandma, to his mother, and an official typed one for him.

He place five of the letters on the hall stand, carrying his own as if it was a piece of delicate pottery into the lounge. He sat in an armchair toying with it, not wanting to know its contents.

Eventually with a resigned sigh, he tore off the corner of the envelop flap, then inserting his finger, split the envelope open. He took out the letter, unfolded it, and spread it out on his knee, deliberately not looking at it. Then after a big intake of breath he looked down, and it was as if he was floating up from his chair. There in bold print it read, 'Surrey County Council are happy to announce that they are making a full grant for tuition fees and maintenance to Andrew Howard during and until the completion of his medical studies'. He almost wept again, "Christ," he said out loud, "I must cut out this blubbing stuff."

The sentence written by Surrey County Council was up to then, the most important sentence he had ever read in his life. It meant that he would not have to depend on his parents for finance, possibly ever again, and perhaps, more important, although his mother was always so snappy at him, this would at least silence some of her heavier guns.

He had never been happier in his whole life. He wanted to shout and sing, but mother was in bed sleeping off her late night from the troop concert.

He made himself some breakfast, tea, Shredded Wheat, toast and marmalade, all with one hand, the other clutching the letter from the County Council which he read and re-read. He wondered whether he would be able to stick it out to be a doctor, but anyway, whatever happened, he had the place in Medical School, and the money to pay for it. It was nearing the end of July, and he was on holiday until early October. All that glorious free time. Perhaps he would try and find Joneson and they could cycle to Blackpool or wherever again. He had three pounds fifteen shillings saved, plus the five pounds his father had given him — the world was his oyster.

At 9.30 a.m., with an impish grin on his face, he brewed a small pot of tea for his mother. It was no good trying to make her toast because it would be too thick, too thin, too much butter or too little butter, and she didn't want marmalade on it anyway, it was spread too thick or too thin, and so on. It was a risk with the tea that carried all the permutations of too strong, too weak, too hot, too cold.

He knocked on her door. She was awake, lost in thought.

Her first words. "It wouldn't hurt you to do this a bit more often Mr Medical Student."

Andy could have predicted word for word exactly what she would say, then on she went.

"It's all right standing there looking pleased with yourself. Who is going to pay for you at the Medical School, who, come on tell me, your father and I have made enough sacrifices for you already?"

Andy handed her the letter from the County Council, all she had said so far really meant nothing, this was how she was. She seemed incapable of ever saying anything nice, yet she took good care of all of them. Andy always had a clean shirt ready, the beds were made, the meals were good, her Sunday lunches unbeatable, her Yorkshire pudding was the best in the world.

She studied the letter for a minute searching for an answer. Then it came.

"This is all very well, but it will be your father and I who have to pay the extras for I don't know how many years."

Andy smiled to himself as she handed the letter back. Thought it wasn't up to her usual standard, perhaps the play had gone well that night. He went down the stairs as his mother drank her tea, then wandered into the town hoping to bump into someone he knew. Life was a bit difficult in this respect. He had deserted the grammar school to go to Metson College where he had only been for two years and one term; arriving too late, and staying too short a time to make lasting friendships. He was neither fish, flesh, fowl, nor good red herring.

Two years and a bit is a long time in a boy's life. The people he had been with at the grammar school had got on with their lives and he was never a public schoolboy, just a grammar school one who had happened to be attending a public school for a couple of years.

He went to Wilson's Café for a coffee. When he had been at the grammar school it was the place where everybody who was anybody went on a Saturday morning. Boys from the grammar school and the girls from the high school throwing eye messages to each other across the room. But now the place was nearly empty. In one corner a boy of his own age, whose face looked vaguely familiar, was entertaining two girls and judging from their giggling and almost hysterical laughter, was being highly successful.

Andy thought he had nodded to him as he sat down, and was reading through the local paper, when the boy came over and sat with him. This looks promising Andy thought. Perhaps he is going to ask me to make a foursome.

The youth said, "Long time no see Andy," then Andy remembered who it was. He couldn't remember his name but he was one of a group of about six who had a masturbation competition whenever the school had to go to the air raid shelters. This youth was invariably the winner.

"Still winning," said Andy.

The youth flushed with pleasure that his prowess had been remembered.

"You bet," he replied, "that's why I have come over, could you let me have a couple of Frenchies? I'm on to a dead cert over there."

Andy wasn't sure that he was too pleased that his place in the scheme of things had been remembered. He knew that he had three in his wallet, but still feeling perverse he said, "Sorry, only one," fishing it out from his wallet under the cover of the café menu.

The youth's face fell. "Never mind, it will wash if I'm careful. Thanks Andy," he said as he got up to go.

"Whoa just a minute," said Andy, "have you seen Joneson lately?"

"Gone on the stage," said the youth edging restlessly towards his girls.

"Ward?" said Andy.

"Don't know him," said the youth.

"Dinga Powell?" said Andy.

"Army," said the youth.

"Paul Mason, John Ranshall?" the youth now almost out of earshot just shook his head.

Andy picked up the local paper again, the lead articles on the front page said nothing. Turning idly to an inner page, he was struck by a large print headline, 'The sheer professionalism of Elsie Howard ensured that *Ladies in Retirement* was an outstanding success at the Bendon Army Camp last night'. Then the article went on to explain how brilliant was his mother, and that she had been a trained professional actress, which in a way, of course, she was.

Andy felt proud and excited. He got up to go, dying to show it to his mother.

As he got up the youth beckoned him over to join them. "Sorry," said Andy, "I'm in a hurry."

He ran all the way home, let himself in through the front door, then shouted excitedly, "Mum, mum."

"There's no need to shout," said his mother, gliding out of the drawing room like a disturbed ghost.

"Look," said Andy, holding out the paper.

"What do I want with that rag," said his mother.

"Just look," said Andy, getting impatient.

His mother looked startled as she turned to her headlines, read the article at least twice, going whiter in the face all the time, and then, for the very first time that Andy could ever remember, she grabbed him in a huge hug and sobbed and sobbed. Christ, thought Andy, we must have weeping in our genes.

Andy did not know how long his mother clung to him, it seemed to be half an hour, but was probably just a few minutes. Suddenly she regained her composure, shook herself, literally, and said, "I'm sorry, you are a good lad," she squeezed his arm and went back to her room.

Suddenly Andy understood a whole range of things. His mother's barrage of words were just a protective screen. Perhaps, before, he'd been too young to appreciate this. Now she had achieved something, it didn't sound much, just a write-up in the local rag, but the important thing was it said that she was a professional actress. He wondered now whether the balance of things between his mother and father would change. He would just have to wait and see.

His mother stayed in her room for the rest of the afternoon and only came downstairs at about 6 o'clock. "Be a good lad and fetch some fish 'n ships," she said in a voice that was quite foreign to Andy. They had just time to eat them before the actors' coach called to pick her up for yet another performance.

His father was working late again and had not yet appeared home.

Andy admired his father greatly, and fully realized the long hours he put in at work. He wondered if his father's colleagues put in anything like the hours his father did. His father seemed to be working later and later every night.

He had kept one portion of fish 'n chips back ready to heat up when his father came in, grumbling, at about 8.30 p.m., looking weary and exhausted.

Poor dad, thought Andy, and for a moment as he looked at his father, he thought he had cut his cheek.

He was about to say something to him, but then, as his father turned away, Andy realized that it wasn't blood or a cut, it was lipstick. He said nothing, but hoped his father would find it when he went upstairs to wash, remove it and then the matter wouldn't come up.

He couldn't bear to think of the consequences, but his working late, and staying on at the office, did now have a new interpretation.

By the time his father came down his face was clean, thank God, and Andy gave him the warmed fish 'n chips, at the same time handing him the local rag with the story of his mother's success.

His father read it, then whistled between his teeth. "So the old girl's hit the headlines. I wonder what she'll be like to live with now?"

Andy, feeling strangely protective towards her, said nothing.

For the next few days Andy looked around trying to find somebody to cycle to Blackpool with him.

Anybody who was almost a friend at Metson College had just sneered at the idea, they were off on their hols to their villas in exotic places like the South of France.

In the end, he could find no one, and when he was reaching this stage he felt strangely cheerful. He was on his own, but that wasn't so bad. He was free, he could go where he liked, stop when he liked, and was glad that no one was going with him.

He was older now than on his last trip, the war had finished, there was no black-out, but still rationing, and more cars on the road.

He still had all his old cycling and camping equipment, but again had to borrow a framed rucksack; his shorts were a bit tight, but were good enough. He had to give his bicycle a good service as it was getting a bit rusty, although the plastic wood handle grips were as good as ever.

He pored over maps to see where he might go, first of all Blackpool, of course, to see his grandma.

In the couple of weeks he had to prepare for his trip there was a quietness in the house he had never experienced before. His parents hardly spoke, it was as if they were almost frightened of each other.

Before it had been the dominant father and the shrewish housewife, and now it was the working father and the actress wife.

Although they hardly spoke it wasn't because there was animosity between them, there was even a relaxed atmosphere. It was quite eerie.

Having collected all his stuff together, Andy set off for Blackpool. It took him a good four days again and was just as hard as it had been the last time, just good old grandma and her high teas with brawn, pressed tongue, potted shrimps, trifle and salad.

He stayed for a week. At the end of the promenade at Squires Gate, he spotted a boy of his own age with a Rugby ball, struck up a friendship and they ran up and down the sands day after day throwing the ball to each other, side stepping imaginary opponents and scoring innumerably unopposed tries. He liked staying with his grandma and grandpa Butcher, his mother's parents. They were said to be as different as chalk and cheese. Andy felt that this was a mistake, and that the saying itself was a mistake. There was many a piece of cheese he had eaten that was almost indistinguishable from chalk, particularly from his mother's larder. To say his mother was frugal was an understatement, nothing edible was ever thrown away. There would be about six resident different dishes with gravy in that might become useful, old mashed potato that could easily be fried up and several jams that only needed the mould scooping off the top to be all right.

Andy himself had once written on the blackboard quite legibly with something hard, which on full examination turned out to be an old piece of cheese.

It was much safer to say his grandparents were very different. They had retired to Blackpool from Sheffield, fulfilling a dream of spending their last days in a bungalow near the sea.

Andy's grandfather had been in banking. He was always referred to as an ex Bank Manager, but he probably had only been a senior clerk, whereas grandma Butcher had been the daughter of a Bank Manager and always felt slightly superior towards her husband.

In Sheffield they had belonged to everything, the Church, the Mothers' Union, the Bowling Club, the Choir, and in younger years the Operatic Society. His grandfather had been treasurer of a dozen clubs or societies. They could not walk down any street in the town without bumping into at least half a dozen people they knew.

They were given a huge retirement party by friends and business associates, with even the Mayor attending, and everyone envying them escaping from the soot and grime of an industrial town to Blackpool and the seaside, and it was not just Blackpool ordinary, they were going to, it was South Shore, Blackpool, and if you put down Squires Gate on a letter addressed to them instead of South Shore, it would reach them and this was almost on a par with living at Lytham St Annes.

They might as well have moved to Siberia.

From being people of importance in Sheffield, they became just an old couple living in a bungalow at Blackpool. Living off the crumbs of visits by their children and grandchildren.

They were always hospitable, and having the family evacuated to stay with them as evacuees during the early part of the war was one of those strange bonuses that wartime sometimes throws up.

One of Andy's happiest pre-war memories was when convalescing after an appendix operation, he had a whole week there on his own, and grandma Butcher had taken him to the pictures in Lytham St Annes to see Jeannette McDonald and Nelson Eddy in technicolour in the film *Smiling Through*. The song *When Those Two Eyes of Blue Come Smiling Through*, he never forgot, and for many years he fantasized about rescuing Jeannette McDonald from situations where no other man than he dared to go.

His grandma Butcher was a very large heavy woman, round, and smelling of powder and perfumes. She was far too large to get into an ordinary bath, so once a fortnight she went by bus to Lytham St Annes for a Turkish bath and a massage.

In later years, Andy used to wonder what it was like for the lucky person who was designated to unpeel, bath and massage her.

His grandfather, on the other hand, was a tiny thin very studious man who only lost his temper if he found that you were sitting reading on the toilet when he was waiting to go in.

He was so thin that one day in bed his hip had got caught in grandma's flowing nightie and tore it.

Every day his grandfather read a book, and every day he went to Boots Library where he was a member, to draw out another book and each and every book was about travel and adventure.

Andy often wondered what went on in this little man's head, as he hardly ever spoke, just sat and read. Was he paddling up the Amazon, climbing Everest, as Andy himself had been rescuing Jeannette McDonald from impossible situations years before?

He must have accumulated a huge fund of knowledge over the years, but he didn't seem able to discuss it, share it, or pass it on. He had always wanted to travel, so a lifetime as a bank clerk in Sheffield was for him akin to keeping a lion in a small metal cage.

As far as Andy was concerned, they were always good to him and spoilt him a bit, and he always enjoyed going there.

His grandmother always cried when he left, whilst his grandfather just looked up from his book and nodded.

Andy left Blackpool wandering down the western route home. Chester, which he marvelled at, Bridgnorth where he camped in a farmer's field and was asked to dinner where they were all very sophisticated, smoked black Russian cigarettes and drank wine. It was very good of them to ask him. They were all in dinner jackets and long dresses and although he was just in shorts and a rough shirt, nobody patronized him, and they all seemed interested in his journey and what he was doing.

He also visited Shrewsbury, Ludlow and came down as far south as Worcester.

He thought it was all quite beautiful. This was the sort of England he had read about in books. He particularly liked the battered regimental flags hanging in the Cathedrals in Chester and

Worcester and wondered what tales they would have to tell if they could speak. From Worcester he managed to make it home in a day, wondering what sort of reception he would receive from his parents.

It was a Saturday, the day he arrived home.

They were both in, but hardly acknowledged his arrival, as they were going at each other hammer and tongs, about nothing. What had happened just before Andy had left home had been a temporary lull in a longstanding war.

Andy sadly put away all his gear and went up to his room, hearing the continual raised voices from downstairs. He had no idea what the issue was. He had a mental picture of ships — men-of-war firing broadsides at one another.

In the mail waiting for him was confirmation that he had accommodation in the student hostel attached to St Jane's Hospital.

He looked forward to leaving the battlefields of home to have a room of his own and independence, but at the same time he had a dreadful sinking feeling in the pit of his stomach. Would he be able to cope as a medical student, and what would be required of him?

CHAPTER 3

DISASTER

Elsie Howard had gone overboard in preparing and equipping Andy for medical school.

A steady pile of clean washed pressed clothes grew in his bedroom. In addition, she had stitched his name label to every article, even handkerchiefs and towels.

"Mum," Andy protested, "I'm going to medical school, not to boarding school."

His mother jerked upright in one of her attacking moods.

"Have you ever lived in the community before," she snapped.

"No," said Andy, "but er."

"There's no but about it," said his mother, "don't give opinions about things you know nothing about."

Andy tried desperately to think of some situation where his mother had lived in the community and gained her experience. He was going to challenge her then thought better of it. What he couldn't see anywhere amongst the piles of clothes and equipment, was his Rugby gear.

"Mum," he said tentatively, "I can't see my Rugby kit anywhere."

"You won't," said his mother, not turning her head. "I want you to give it up. You played far too much Rugby at that expensive college you went to. If you'd spent more time studying, you might have done better."

Andy nearly exploded. He had one of his strange energy surges. He gripped his mother's shoulder, his face almost touching hers, and in a loud, but controlled voice, he said, "The only reason I got into St Jane's was because I had my first XV colours. If I'd played for

Surrey or England I would have had a Scholarship. Even if I didn't want to play Rugby, which I do, I would have to at St Jane's, everybody has. Please find my kit now, if you've got rid of them," he broke into a sweat at the thought, "Dad will have to buy me some more tomorrow."

His mother was staggered by the authority and the force of this boy man she had brought into the world. She looked and was scared of the situation she had created.

She shrugged his hand off her shoulder, snarling in defiance. "That," she said, "is absolutely disgusting. Do you mean to tell me that to be a doctor first of all you have to be good at rolling in the mud? In fact, I've never heard of anything so disgusting."

She had regained her composure now.

"If that's the way you feel," she said, "you can get yourself ready for this precious medical school."

"Mum," said Andy, his voice still raised, "where are my Rugby things?"

"Find them if you can," said his mother, and stalked out of the room.

Andy searched the house from top to bottom. There should have been his boots, almost new; two pairs of shorts, one white one blue; two pairs of 1st XV socks; one pair of 2nd XV socks; one 1st XV shirt and one house XV shirt. You couldn't just hide them anywhere. He had only seen them yesterday, she hadn't had time to send them to a jumble, she couldn't have burnt them, but where? Then he had a thought, dismissed it, then thought he had better make sure — the dustbin. The top was filled with broken egg shells, tea leaves, and old newspapers, then he saw a piece of cloth, pulled it, and yes it was his Rugby bag with all his kit in. 'God,' he thought, 'if I'd have waited until tomorrow the dustmen would have had them.'

Andy's mother ignored him as he walked in with his kit, and made a point of not speaking to him for the rest of the day. The next morning, however, she was busy ironing and packing for him, just as if nothing had happened.

Both his mother and father drove with him to the Medical School that evening. It was the closest that Andy had felt to them.

His mother almost on good terms with his father, but of course, a back seat driver. "You're going too fast, mind that cyclist, d'you know you almost went through a red light there?" But overall it was a bit subdued, they were a bit subdued, their lives were going to change. For the first time his mother and father would be alone together. Andy felt a mixture of anxiety and excitement, and despite all its battles, he would miss home.

They arrived at the Medical School Hostel, some converted houses in what was once a fashionable London area, now much down-market, but only 400 yards from the hospital. Nobody has ever found the mythical elephant graveyard where they go to die, this area was noted as the one in which all the old prostitutes came to die. Looking at the battered wrecks lining the street Andy estimated that their average age was about eighty, and wondered who would want to touch them.

There were about six other families unloading sons or daughters as they arrived at the Hostel; a few parents a bit red eyed. "Huh," snorted Andy's mother, "I had no idea that the accommodation was mixed, that will lead to no good." Andy's father gave him a grin and a wink.

Andy's mother inspected his room and the common rooms, sweeping round imperiously looking for dust traces. She ran her finger over the top of pictures and skirtings, with Andy and his father following behind.

"She's playing Queen Victoria," said his father."

The rooms were arranged in groups of four, each room had a desk with a chair, chest of drawers, wardrobe, single bed, and a wash basin. An easy chair with an overhead light was by the bed and an angle poise lamp on the desk. The four rooms shared a common bathroom with a bath and shower and a kitchen with electric stove, sink and four storage cupboards.

There was a row of clothes washing machines. One glance at them by his mother was enough, "Don't go playing with those," she said, "bring your washing home."

There was also a large common room, a small TV room and a bar in an alcove off the large common room. There were three or four superior looking youths at the bar clasping great pints in one hand and looking contemptuously at all these new people unloading and weeping, or both. Forgetting that it was only a year ago when they were in exactly the same situation.

Andy's mother laboriously unpacked and stored away his clothes, and then took a cardboard box full of tins, jars of jams and marmalade, coffee, tea, and condensed milk and arranged them all neatly in his individual kitchen cupboard.

They returned to his room now, all a bit awkward with one another.

His father sat in the easy chair blowing his nose, his mother sat on the bedside, Andy stood impatiently wanting to be off to explore on his own, but at the same time, not really wanting them to go.

"Well, we'd better be off," said his father in a strange sort of husky voice, and with obvious signs that he had enlisted in the red-eyed brigade. His mother, as if loath to leave, made one more final inspection of everything, keeping her face away from the two men.

When she turned round, to Andy's surprise there were tears running down her face, she accepted his embrace warmly. This was only the second time that he ever remembered warmth and embrace from his mother, the other time being when she saw her write-up in the local rag.

A quite different mother from usual said, "Please don't go and disappear like your sister Lettice."

"Of course I won't," said Andy, "I'll phone, and it's going to be a giant who will have to stop me coming home for Sunday lunch."

His father just shook his hand, too choked to speak and by now at least a sergeant major in the red-eyed brigade and, so they went.

The next two weeks for Andy couldn't have been fuller. There was a Freshers Party, where everybody was friendly, and hundreds of societies to join or not to join. He had his first introduction to the dissecting room, where formalin preserved bodies bore no relation to human beings, and were to be his constant companions for the next two years.

As part of an introductory course, like animated penguins in their short white coats, they were given a tour of the Hospital proper, wards, operating theatre, and out-patients. They almost felt like doctors, nodding to patients as they walked through the wards. Life was absolutely tremendous. He had no idea that it could be so good. He had meant to go home on his second weekend, but no one else was, and there was so much to do that he rang his parents, and though they both said they fully understood, they did sound disappointed.

The Rugby was exciting with nearly everybody playing, and the teams took a great deal of sorting out. There was a shortage of hookers, and Andy finished up by being selected for the extra 'A' XV, which wasn't bad for a start, as they were the gods of the 1st XV. The whippets, which was really the name for the 2nd XV, the 'A' XV, the extra 'A' XV, the 'B' XV, the extra 'B' XV, the 'C' XV and the School's XV, which was a bit of a mixture of all seven playing the top Rugby schools mid-week.

Not a great beer drinker, Andy had to down his pints with the rest. On their train journey back from a game in Bedford, full of beer at the end of Andy's second week as a student, rolling drunkenly around in their railway compartment, somehow they managed to smash a window, which meant calling the guard. The guard called the railway police, who took all their names and the name of their medical school. It was far more sobering than any egg flip.

"Forget it," said an experienced clinical student, "nothing will happen," but Andy couldn't forget about it, and worried about it all over the weekend.

He was not in the least surprised to be summoned from the physiology lecture on the Monday morning by a porter with a message that the Dean wanted to see him in his office urgently.

Andy was puzzled that he was the only one sent for, as there were at least three people from the same fracas attending the lecture.

He made his way nervously to the Dean's study. The Dean, who had interviewed him, had retired, and this was a new broom Dean, a neurologist. He had already thrown out two of the Medical School's Rugby internationals as he felt that ten years was too long a period to spend at a Medical School getting a degree.

Andy felt that it was terribly unfair for just him to be there. He was in fact sitting down when the window was broken, perhaps they were going to see the others later.

In a few minutes the Dean's secretary called him into the office. He was surprised when the Dean got up from his desk, shook his hand and said, "Come and sit down Andy," pointing to a large leather upholstered chair. The Dean returned to his desk.

"Andy," he said in the kindest of voices, "unfortunately I have some very bad news for you. The coach your mother was travelling in to a troop concert last night was involved in a traffic accident. Sadly four of the cast, of whom your mother was one, were killed instantly.

"I am so sorry to have to be the bearer of such sad news, but please be assured that everyone here will help in any way possible."

CHAPTER 4

DR ANDREW HOWARD

Andy stared out of the train window as he made his way home. The Dean had said how well he had taken the awful news, but he had done nothing of the sort. All the Dean had done was say some words, words don't mean anything. He could not believe that his mother had been killed. He felt sure that it was a mistake. He just wished the train would hurry, and he could see for himself. Oh why hadn't he made the effort to go down at the weekend and, as he became impatient with himself he kicked his bag and a sense of realization began to dawn.

Setting off for home he had automatically stuffed his bag with his dirty clothes as his mother had instructed. Suddenly he knew she was dead, this was what death meant. There would be no one to wash his clothes, no more Sunday dinners, and no more Yorkshire puddings. He felt his heart was going to burst.

When he thought of his mother he could only think of the good things about her, the way she had taken care of him. The words she spat out meant nothing; words don't mean anything.

He now realized how upset and hurt she must have been when his sister Lettice disappeared from their lives. He was only aware of this when she said goodbye to him at the hostel. In his imagination he saw her with Lettice as the first adored baby, then the little girl in pretty frocks, school, parties, party dresses, boys, one eyed Joe — then gone, without a backward glance.

He wept inwardly for her. Thank God she'd had that write-up in the local paper. The local rag was probably more important to her than a national daily.

He wondered how his father would be. He felt anger towards him.

His parents always rowed bitterly and he knew that his father had extramarital adventures. Perhaps his father would be glad that his mother had died, freeing him to go off with whoever it was that he dallied with in the evenings.

He was determined to be deliberately cool with him when they met.

The train journey seemed endless, but at last they reached his home station. His father was waiting in his car just outside. Andy threw his bag in the back of the car then walked round to the front and got inside beside his father. They looked at each other, wound their arms round each other and wept.

Home was not the chaos he thought it would be. The table was set for lunch. The widow from next door, whose name Andy couldn't remember, seemed to be bustling around in charge.

"I'll see to these," she said, taking Andy's washing. "You go and sit with your father until lunch is ready."

Her name came back to Andy, Mrs Robinson. She had always been a widow as far as he could remember. She knew his mother quite well, but they'd always vaguely despised her in a way that family groups do to people who are on their own.

"Ooh look at Mrs so-and-so trying to muscle in on things, there's something odd about her you know."

People are in some ways like animals, throwing oddities out of the herd. Very nice people do it, but that's how things are.

But now Mrs Robinson was a ministering angel, quiet and almost birdlike. After the years of being unwanted, almost unnecessary, she was wanted and useful and she was determined to make the best job of it she could while it lasted.

Andy still felt that his mother would come round the corner of the door at any moment.

After lunch they had to get down to the serious business of funerals. His mother's GP called and drew some complicated graphs of patterns of life which were meant to be a comfort, but neither Andy or his father had the faintest idea what he was getting at. Andy wondered privately whether the GP fully understood himself. He had probably taken notes at a bereavement lecture and got them muddled.

The phone rang constantly. Fortunately Mrs Robinson took all the calls, filtering through the important ones.

A man in a black car wearing a black tie hovered at the gate.

"Must be the undertaker," said his father.

They went to the window and beckoned him, the man seemed slightly surprised, but pleased.

Andy met him at the door.

"Do come in," said Andy.

"No that's all right, sir," said the man. "I have just called to say that we are tarmacadaming a bit down the road and we've got some to spare and I could give you a good price for your drive."

"No thank you," said Andy, "we've just had a death in the family, and we thought you were the undertaker." This sent the man scuttling off apologizing.

Andy's mother was one of four people killed, but he could not think beyond his own mother's death, and they made no active steps to get in touch with the families who had also been bereaved.

His father was obviously determined to make up in the funeral for many of the things that he had failed to do for his wife during her life. Andy thought he would be the one running around to the funeral director, registering the death, arranging everything, but his father insisted on doing everything himself and remained poised and calm.

The undertaker was charming and helpful. It was a question of putting notices in papers, type of coffin, type of hearse, and how many cars, et cetera.

Andy's mother had been taken to the Chapel of Rest. As the undertaker was leaving Andy walked alongside him and asked if he could possibly go and see his mother in the Chapel of Rest. "I can only advise you not to sir," said the undertaker.

"I am a medical student," said Andy.

"I'm afraid, sir, I can only really advise you not to."

Andy had no idea how much his mother had been smashed up in the crash, but he had a sudden thought of seeing her as one of the formalized dissecting specimens they were working on in the Medical School.

They had to fix up the time of the funeral service with a young Curate, and as they weren't churchgoers he seemed a bit offhand that they should want an elaborate church service, but nevertheless he was patient with them, and agreed to give her the full works.

Letters started to pour in from everywhere, and the phone was ringing continually for the next few days.

Grandma and Grandpa Butcher came to stay. Grandma was in a terrible state, grandpa said nothing, only looking enviously at a row of books.

There was so much going on, people coming and going.

Mrs Robinson had organized a sort of high tea for the long distance relatives, and after the funeral there would be a glass of sherry for everybody.

Examining the funeral arrangements, Andy was appalled to find that his father had been in touch with the Army Camp that the drama troupe were on their way to. They'd not only had a promise from the Commanding Officer for an Army escort and a firing party, but also the regimental brass band.

Andy just had no time to think or reflect about his mother, most of his reflecting time had been on the train. He still wasn't sure that she was dead, but she must be, there was his father going on as if their marriage had been a love affair akin to Antony and Cleopatra.

The funeral day came, thank God it wasn't raining. It was a reasonably fine autumn day, the Army band played, the Church was packed and, of course, with the soldiers and the band and all the fuss literally hundreds came. The Church, which could hold 600 or 700, was completely full, and crowds had gathered outside. It was all so unreal, more like a pageant than a funeral.

Andy just wanted to get away and grieve quietly.

The Curate did a good job in spite of the fact that he didn't know any of them.

The guard of honour fired a volley over the grave and the band played some sort of funeral march, both there, and as they left the churchyard.

About 30 close relatives and friends filled the house, all jabbering away as if it was a party rather than a funeral. Cousins, aunts, and uncles who hadn't seen each other for years, consuming sandwiches, sausage rolls, trifles and such things.

There was a queue for the two toilets in the house, and fortunately Mrs Robinson had the foresight to get in some extra toilet rolls.

Finally there was a hard core composed of one of his aunts, his grandparents, Andy and his father and Mrs Robinson sitting talking. For the first time they were really talking about his mother. Grandma Butcher, head bowed, weeping steadily into her handkerchief, and Grandpa Butcher, with no book, just sitting looking ahead, and not contributing to the conversation. In the end it was just his grandparents and he and his father, Mrs Robinson had gone home. Then there seemed nothing to talk about. All conversation had been used up.

The next day his father ran the Butchers to the train for them to make the long and tedious journey back to Blackpool, then he took Andy up to the cemetery.

His mother's grave was covered with a mound of wreaths and flowers. His father was strangely silent.

They drove home and there was Mrs Robinson bustling around again, flitting, would have been a more appropriate word, but everything was neat and tidy, everything was washed up. There were some sandwiches on the table.

Andy's father said, "I'm just nipping upstairs for a bit," and, to his surprise, Andy could hear him sobbing.

He thought of the constant warfare that had gone on between his parents over the years.

Why was he crying now she was gone?

For no reason, Andy's mind suddenly flashed back to the time when he was at the Grammar School and in a boxing match where he and his opponent were so shagged out that they leant against each other. They had got applause for good sportsmanship, whereas, they were so tired that that was the only way they could stay on their feet.

He realized that the continual battle that went on between his parents, really held them in balance against each other, and with one gone it left his father to fall on his face. In spite of all the words that had been flung about for so many years, perhaps he had been a good enough husband and perhaps she had been a good enough wife and mother. She had certainly looked after them.

Andy walked into town to a stationers, and bought a couple of books of leaf type photograph albums where you slide in photographs and they stick up like a pack of cards, each containing about sixty photos. He then went through all the drawers and desks in the house looking for photographs of his mother, slotting them into his new purchases.

Having finished, he took them up to his room and carefully studied the hundred or so photographs he had collected. On nearly every one she was smiling. Could she really have had a happy life?

Tears ran down Andy's cheeks, then, like his father, he turned on his bed and wept.

He stayed another week at home with his father, and they seemed at ease with each other, and Mrs Robinson seemed to be almost a permanent fixture.

Andy was pleased she was unobtrusive, spotless and a good cook, although she couldn't make Yorkshire pudding like his mother, and her Sunday lunches weren't nearly as good, but they weren't bad. Perhaps she'd take care of his father, unless he had other ideas about his future.

It was possible that he already had a partner lined up, but this didn't seem obvious in the way he behaved during the week of the funeral.

At the end of the second week since the day of his mother's death, Andy said he would have to be getting back to medical school.

His father nodded in agreement and said, "Well I expect I must get back to work as well."

On the Sunday he drove Andy to the station, he had been away from the medical school for two weeks but it seemed like two years.

When he got back everything had been going on apace, and everybody seemed settled and had got on with their studies, their games, their clubs and their associations.

He felt like a stranger coming into the hostel. The others all seemed like old hands with Andy being the only new boy.

When he got back to the physiology department and the anatomy department he was a full two weeks behind everybody and he never caught up.

It took Andy a month to settle back into the hospital and medical school life. He still felt slightly apart from the others, principally because he knew less than anybody else. Being away for two weeks meant that he had lost his place in the Extra 'A' XV and was now a hooker of the 'B' XV where the Rugby was more social than enthusiastic. In the 'B' XV he could almost guarantee that he would hook the ball from 95% of the scrums, whoever put the ball in.

So the autumn term drifted on. He went home every Sunday for lunch to keep his father company. Mrs Robinson was a permanent fixture nowadays, coming in each morning and taking care of things. It was purely a business arrangement, and without being unkind, you only had to take one look at Mrs Robinson to know that it could have only been a business arrangement. She was a tremendous boon to them and, of course, they were a tremendous boon to her. Once again in her life she mattered.

"I see that you are living symbiotically with Mrs Robinson," Andy said to his father.

"No, there's nothing like that," said his father, looking affronted.

"Symbiosis," said Andy, "is a physiological situation where two organisms both benefit by associating with each other."

"Huh," said his father, "don't get clever medical with me."

His father had changed since his mother died. The flurry of trying to make up after her death for what he hadn't done when she was alive had died down. Andy was pretty sure that his father had given up his extramarital flings and just solidly grieved for his sparring partner. Andy had once read in some literary work, and he had a feeling that it was to do with King Arthur and his lot, that marriage means obedience, and that romance was outside marriage by definition. Now this father had no longer a safe castle to retire to there was no point in going out and romancing.

Andy grieved for his mother, and grieved particularly for how his relationship with her might have been very different, and it was only in the last couple of months of her life that he had seen flashes of it.

The medical school term eventually finished. The last fixture of the 'B' XV was played on the main hospital pitch as a curtain raiser to the 1st XV's game and some mixture of fixtures. Instead of the 'B' XV of the other club appearing, they had send their 'A' XV, and they were huge.

There was also an ever increasing crowd coming in to see the main match.

It was decided to go ahead with the mismatch to give both sides a run out, and the 'B' XV, playing before a crowd for the first time, excelled themselves. They tackled and fought like demons, even

Andy, and, although they lost to the superior size and skill of their opponents, they did not disgrace themselves, and in fact gave them a hard game. In one department, the scrums, of course, they were better than their opponents, with Andy winning 75%, even when they were being bundled back by this much bigger side.

Andy did not stay on for the end of term parties. It was all too near his mother's death. He went home and worked at the Post Office during the holidays, then for Christmas Day and Boxing Day he and his father drove up to Blackpool to have Christmas with the Butchers. It was all understandingly dismal. It was a relief to get back home and to Mrs Robinson, and only when they were back home did they realize they hadn't asked Mrs Robinson what she was doing for Christmas. Now it was too late to ask, but it was almost certain that she'd spent it on her own.

Andy went back to the medical school early. His Post Office job had finished at Christmas. He hoped a week in the library might help him catch up. Christmas Day had been on a Monday. He went back on the Thursday evening to find the hostel almost empty. He spent Friday in the library studying anatomy books, which he hated. He had the communal kitchen to himself in the evening and had a huge fry-up followed by Christmas pudding and mince pies that Mrs Robinson had sent him off with.

He went to bed early with a book and the wireless, intending to sleep late, but was woken at 7.30 a.m. by a banging on his bedroom door.

He shouted, "Come in," and in came a very harassed looking secretary of the 1st XV — one of the gods.

"Are you the chap who hooked for the 'B' XV in the game before Christmas?" he said to Andy.

"Yes," said Andy.

"Well quick, get your kit together, you're playing for the 1st XV against Cardiff, the train goes in 30 minutes, our hooker is in the hospital having his appendix out, you are all we've got."

Andy couldn't believe it, but it was true.

At Paddington Station he felt sure that he had seen a very smartly dressed Joneson on an adjacent platform, but there was no time for dallying.

He scrummed down with two huge prop forwards in the area

between the two toilets on the London to Cardiff train to get used to them, then the scrum half came with the ball and they practised timing.

What surprised Andy was that all these Rugby gods were ordinary very nice people, they included three full Rugby internationals, two international trial players, six county players and two war-time international caps.

Cardiff Arms Park in those days was not the magnificent stadium it is today. It doubled as a greyhound racing track and bursts of applause from the crowd were always accompanied by barking by the hundred or so dogs kennelled under the stand.

The game was far quicker than anything Andy could have imagined, he could barely arrive at each scrum in time. Twice they had to wait for him, but he was more than holding his own against the current Welsh international hooker.

Although the hospital lost a good game, 23–20, it established Andy as the 1st XV hooker for the next six years. For the last four he was the team secretary, which meant actually being club secretary, sorting out all the hospital's seven Rugby sides, transport, tours, et cetera.

For the first time in his life he stayed in a hotel, and for the first time he went abroad to play in France. He played twice for Middlesex County, he was revered as one of the Rugby gods by his fellow students, doctors and even consultants, only Andy knew that he wasn't.

It meant that it took him a year longer to qualify than he should have done, and that was hurriedly as an Apothecary, after failing his degree finals.

He would have left the hospital with a great reputation if it had not been for that fateful game against the London Irish in the Twickenham seven-a-sides.

Andy looked back over his medical student days. By and large he had enjoyed them. He always had two underlying layers of anxiety relating to his studies, with which he was always behind, and the other, that although he wore the mantle of being one of the Rugby gods, and was acknowledged as one, he knew he wasn't.

To make up for it he took on every possible activity that he could to support the Rugby club. He was the club and first team secretary for four years, normally the term for this job was one. This meant that he had to see to the laundering of the team shirts and socks, travel by either bus or train and arrange hotel accommodation for Devon and Cornwall tours. For French tours he had to check ferry tickets, see that everybody had a passport, as well as arranging trains or bus travel to France. In addition he had to make the travel arrangements for the other six teams the hospital turned out every week.

On one Cornish tour, when a game was eventually stopped by rain, he actually washed all the 15 muddy shirts in the communal bath when the others had left.

He volunteered to work behind the bar at the first Rugby Club Ball in his first year. He became a regular fixture there, and as he was good at it, in time he also did the bar for the Balls held by the Football Club, the Cricket Club, the Hockey Club and he fixed both bands and bar for the New Year's Eve Ball. In fact he attended just about every Ball held in the six and a half years he was a student, but only from behind the bar. He wanted to be thought of as "Good Old Andy".

Apart from a couple of trips to the pictures with nurses, he never really got entangled with the opposite sex.

He was neither bright nor industrious with his medical studies,. He failed his degree M.B., B.S. twice and only with the coaching by friends did he scrape through the Diploma of the Society of the Apothecaries L.M.S.S.A., which meant he was licensed to practise medicine.

The Society of Apothecaries is one of the ancient livery companies and as well as allowing Andy to practise medicine it also gave him the right to drive sheep or moor his horse or something in the City of London. It was supposed to be easier than the degree M.B., B.S. or the Conjoint Diploma M.R.R.C.S., L.R.C.P. although the midwifery was harder, but it was looked down on as if it was something inferior.

If Andy had got either his Degree or the Conjoint Diploma he could have had the pick of jobs at his Teaching Hospital, just because of his bloody Rugby. All he had failed to pass was the medicine in his degree finals, each time easily passing his obstetrics, gynaecology and surgery, but with just his L.M.S.S.A. he had to look further afield for a job. He finally completed his M.B., B.S. when he was doing a mixed Senior House Officer job of Orthopaedics, Plastics, Ear Nose and Throat, Eyes Dermatology, Venereology, which included a ward full of girls from Holloway Prison suffering from some aspect of this disease.

It made no difference at all to his ability as a doctor, but without it he would have had an inferiority complex for the rest of his working life.

What he had unconsciously learnt with his bar work, his travel and his tour work was to deal with people, how to handle people, and how to make things work. And this was proved a good number of years later when he settled in general practice. If there were four doctors on duty and the surgery was packed with people, three quarters of them would be waiting to see Andy and they wouldn't budge until they had.

The unexpected thing, during his student days, was that he missed his mother terribly, and he later found that he always did.

CHAPTER 5

INTO THE WORKHOUSE

It was late May, and Andy had decided to devote most of the morning in the Medical School library to pore through the job section of the *British Medical Journal*, although he did not know where to begin. The turn-around dates of junior house jobs of which it was essential to do two six month spells, to become a fully registered medical practitioner were the 1st July and the 1st January.

He knew that with only an L.M.S.S.A. qualification all the teaching hospitals were out. He wanted to remain near London, but the only options seemed to be Wigan, Scunthorpe or industrial areas in Wales. He put his *BMJ* back on the magazine rack and wandered off to the Medical School office.

The Medical School was run by a bunch of pretty girls who all ended up marrying doctors, and were overseen by the Secretary of the Medical School, the plump, jovial, Mary Scott, MBE, who had acted as mother, father confessor, shoulder to cry on, and chief Rugby fan of the school for three decades.

Andy went into her office and found her seated behind mounds of forms and books.

"Cheer up Andy," she said. "You look as if you've just had an offer from the Rugby League and it's not big enough."

"That's an idea," said Andy.

"Mary, where on earth do I find a House Physician job in London with my qualifications?"

Mary thought for a minute, dived through a lot of papers, then came up with one headed 'St Daniel's Hospital' with a list of jobs available in every branch and every grade of medicine and surgery.

"Have you tried there?" she said.

"No," said Andy, "where on earth is it, I've never heard of it?"

"Notting Hill," said Mary, "are you interested?"

"Yes," said Andy, "that's only a spitting distance. How is it that I haven't heard of it before, and do you think I would have a chance there, the situation is ideal?"

"Go out and leave it to me," said Mary, but she said, "if you do get a job there, you must promise me that you will sit your degree again and report in from time to time, and don't stay at this hospital for too long."

Andy went out and sat with the girls, which was no hardship. He wondered whether they had been selected because of their looks rather than their ability. He would have had to have been at least a middle grade registrar to have attracted any real attention, but as a Rugby player, they did talk to him, but about Rugby of course.

In about ten minutes Mary called him back in. "You have an appointment with Dr Ramsden the Consultant Physician at 4 p.m. this afternoon."

"You are a wonder woman," said Andy, pecking her on the cheek.

"Well, don't count your chickens," said Mary, "and think it all over carefully."

He was a bit puzzled by that, but hurried back to the hostel to iron a shirt, and press his only suit. Looking at the map he found that St Daniel's Hospital was not strictly Notting Hill, but its tube station and that of Ladbrook Grove were the nearest transport to it. It was an area he knew nothing about.

He left the hospital at half past two, arriving at Notting Hill at three, then, with a street map in hand, set off for St Daniel's. The further he got from Notting Hill the greater the decline in the condition and upkeep of the houses. He passed from smart arty coloured decorated houses to row upon row of what at one time must have been smart Georgian houses, now in the later stages of decay with sagging balconies, peeling paint and boarded up windows. When he at last saw a huge red building in the distance he began to feel as if some time capsule had landed him in a foreign land. There was not a white face to be seen. The dilapidated houses were literally teaming with happy smiling West Indians. Music was drifting out of most of them, groups of children playing in the street and lots of men chatting on the pavement, all acknowledging him with a smile and a "Hi there man".

This was 1953 and he later learnt that this was the main receiving area for West Indian immigrants. He guessed there must have been about sixty people per house. The following Christmas, when one of the hospital porters insisted he came to his home for a drink, he found there was more like thirty to a room. He was introduced to the beaming fat Greek landlord.

In the room he was offered a drink. In one corner there was a woman cooking over a stove, a dozen children were grouped round a flickering TV set, four men were playing cards, and in another corner, on a bed, two women were restraining a third who had obviously had more than her rum ration for the day, but they were all happy.

As Andy approached the red building his heart began to sink. It was as dilapidated as the surrounding houses, and looked like an old Victorian workhouse, which was exactly what it had been.

The hospital was dismal, the only thing about it that wasn't, were the West Indian porters, cleaners and ward maids. They all seemed to think that all was well with the world.

The hospital was in much greater need of a builder, painter and decorator than a House Physician.

He was interviewed by Dr Ramsden the Consultant Physician, a rather tall, stern man, and Mr Farrant the Medical Superintendent, an affable surgeon. There was no real interview, both men looked harassed and just asked him when he could start.

"Oh, oh, the 1st July," said Andy surprised.

Their faces fell. "Any chance of the 1st June?" said Dr Ramsden, "We're a bit short."

"Certainly," said Andy. It all seemed to be too easy. Mary Scott must have put a lot of spade work in for him.

"Whilst you are here," said Mr Farrant, "see the Head Porter and choose a room, as Dr Ramsden said, we're a bit short of junior staff at present."

"What's the full complement?" asked Andy.

"Oh, eighteen," said the two almost in unison, and rather nervously, "but we do have a full complement of Registrars and Senior Registrars."

Andy was so excited about landing the job so easily, he hadn't taken enough notice of what they'd said.

The Head Porter was a tall loose limbed relaxed Jamaican. "Hi man," he said. "So you want a room. You're lucky, I have the best room for you. It may not look the best room but it is, and as a bonus you have Miss World for your neighbour. She won't speak to you, but, yes sir, she sure is Miss World."

He led Andy off through the battered building to an archway where some stone steps led up to a small landing with three doors leading off. "That's her ladyship's," said the porter pointing to the right hand door and, as if on cue, a woman who looked as if she'd just stepped out of Vogue swept out, completely ignored the two and tripped off down the stairs.

"Phew," said Andy, "who and what is she?"

"That," said the porter, "is Miss World, otherwise Miss Diane Reynolds, Senior Surgical Registrar. Now, if you're still here in six months she still won't speak to you, she has her own bath, bedroom and sitting room. That's your bathroom and toilet," pointing to the room ahead.

Andy looked in to see a rusty bath, chipped wash basin and broken toilet seat. "Lovely," he said.

"Now," said the porter. "the master bedroom." He opened the door and Andy's heart sank. It was a large shabby room, with a single bed in one corner and a telephone on a bedside table. The plaster from the ceiling was down in the far corner. There was a battered old armchair, a chest of drawers and wardrobe even more battered still. A modern small pine table with two upright chairs and a gas fire with an old-fashioned gas ring. The floor was covered with linoleum with a rug by the bed and one by the gas fire.

"What is your name?" Andy asked the Head Porter.

"They call me O'Sullivan, man," said the Head Porter.

"What O'Sullivan," said Andy.

"Just O'Sullivan," said the porter.

"Why O'Sullivan," said Andy.

"Because I'm Irish," said the porter.

"What part of Ireland," said Andy laughing.

"Why, the Jamaican part," said the porter grinning.

"Well, Irish," said Andy, "what about showing me a proper room?"

"Man," said Irish, "this is the best room. That gas ring could have been made of gold, you can make cocoa, soup, heat up beans, it's the only one — wait till you taste this hospital food."

"This really is the best resident's room in the hospital? Fine, Irish," said Andy, "if this is the best room, why haven't one of the other housemen taken it?"

"Well," said Irish, grinning, "the other two housemen, are a boy and a girl and they are very very good friends and they have two rooms close together."

"What do you mean?" said Andy, "the other two, they told me there was a complement of eighteen."

"Yeah, man," said Irish, "I expect they also said they're just a wee bit short of junior staff at present."

"Yes," said Andy, puzzled.

"What they meant, man," said Irish, "was that they were fifteen short."

"Christ," said Andy, "I'm signed up for six months now."

"Don't worry," said Irish, "people come and go, we could perhaps have eight by next week, or it could just be you. Lots of people seem to go rather than come." Andy's heart sank. "Don't worry," said Irish, "you've got a damn fine registrar. Dr Hudson, he sure is the best doctor in the place."

Irish took Andy on a conducted tour of the hospital. It was a huge old Victorian workhouse, and although Andy was dismayed at the state of the building, he had a sneaking admiration for the Victorians who managed to build these huge buildings for the poor. St Daniel's had 600 beds, 300 were for patients with tuberculosis. Andy thought, that's 200 patients for each houseman. He was interrupted by Irish who said, "You don't have to work with the Consumptives, they have their own team."

'Good,' thought Andy, that means just 100 each.

The wards all looked very much the same, all in need of refurbishment. The nursing staff seemed strangely subdued, ward sisters just nodding as they were introduced.

"What's the matter, Irish?" said Andy, "are they all waiting for the guillotine?"

"No," said Irish, "they're waiting for her majesty to come round."

"Come on, Irish," said Andy, "I know the Queen isn't coming."

"She's here man," said Irish stiffly. "you'll have to stand to attention."

A squat square faced woman in a dark blue uniform with a white creation like a small bell tent on her head, swept into the ward. She was followed by three simpering minions in dark green uniforms with mini hike tents on their heads, the sides of the tent to the front.

"What are you doing here O'Sullivan, and who is this man?" boomed the lady. Even O'Sullivan looked overawed.

He stuttered, "This is doctor ..." then looked helplessly at Andy for the name.

"I'm Dr Ramsden's new House Physician, Andrew Howard," said Andy, stepping forward proffering a hand.

The matron ignored his proffered hand, pointed a pencil at him in a sort of stabbing movement accompanied by a growl like a sergeant major and said, "Housemen do not drink tea or coffee on the wards, if they want refreshment, they go to the Doctors' Mess." She then turned on her heel and set off down the ward accompanied by her following troupe.

"Quick, let's go," said Irish.

When they got into the main corridor Irish said, "If she ever found you smoking on the ward you'd be shot at dawn. If anyone could arrange a fight between her and Joe Louis, I'd back her."

The tour of the hospital/workhouse was all very depressing, although he was cheered to find a diminutive Polish lady registrar who ran Casualty and was nice and friendly. She and Irish were the only two people he had met who had even been reasonable.

Irish walked out to the hospital gate with him. "Don't worry," said Irish, "you'll be all right, I'll keep an eye on you, I am always there if you want me. I'm the most discreet man you'll ever meet, just one bottle of whisky will seal my lips forever." They slapped palms at the gate. "See you Monday," said Irish.

"Perhaps," said Andy, then with his head down, he trudged off to the Notting Hill tube.

CHAPTER 6

A DIP INTO THE WELL OF PLEASURE

Andy soon found that he loved being a doctor. The first three months of his House Physician's job were tremendous. He had never worked harder in his life, but he enjoyed it. Nights and weekends were terrible, they were so understaffed. The Path Lab closed at weekends, so the Housemen had to cross-match any blood needed, as well as all their other tasks. Fortunately, as O'Sullivan had forecast, the number of resident staff increased. Two hard-working girls and a lazy lunatic man from St Jane's were the first to join the team. The lunatic man was really a lunatic, he would be half-way through putting a plaster of Paris on say a broken leg, notice it was knocking-off time and just go off and leave it.

They were followed by a sort of united nations, two Indians, one Nigerian, one Irishman, one Lebanese, one Pole and a young Scottish anaesthetist. They all used to gather in Andy's room for 9 o'clock cocoa made on the precious gas ring and swap experiences.

The Pole, who had lived in the part of Poland occupied by the Russians in 1939, had been transported by them to a camp in Mongolia for two years. He told them that the Mongolians had not only never heard of Poland or England, they'd never even heard of Russia. Then when Germany invaded Russia, they were transported to the Middle East to join the Polish Army.

They were a happy lot, and O'Sullivan, or one of his contemporaries, always knew where people were if an emergency arose.

Andy suffered with getting too close to his patients, as he did throughout his medical life. He had a thirty-five-year-old man with a stroke, slowly getting better to the delight of his wife who was the maid in some wealthy household. Andy would talk to her every day and to her employers who visited occasionally. The young man was almost ready to go home, when one night he had a pulmonary embolism and died within twenty-four hours.

Andy had to break the news to his wife who was quite hysterical. He was almost as upset as she was, but somehow had not to show it, as well as to comfort her. He felt somehow that it was his fault.

Andy's pay at the time was fifteen pounds a month. A couple of weeks after the death of the young man, he got a thank you letter from the wife with a ten pound note which was probably two months' wages for her.

Andy groaned, "Ten pounds, and a husband who died under my care."

It took him weeks to come to terms with this particular death, and from then on he was anxious when anybody was recovering, and about to go home, to make a careful examination of their lower legs to see if there was any evidence of a deep vein thrombosis.

Apart from his own work under his own Physician and Registrar, he was called to all ends of the hospital, giving anaesthetic in Casualty, or helping out there with a bit of stitching up. On his first night on duty he was called to an emergency on the Thoracic Surgery Ward, his heart sank, he knew nothing about thoracic surgery. He approached the ward nervously, there were about half a dozen men in beds with drips, tubes, oxygen tents and large blood stained Winchester drainage bottles on the floor. This was today's list and all had either lost a lung or at least half a lung.

He was approached by the efficient-looking male charge nurse who said, "Sorry to bother you doctor, but the suction drainage from number two bed is not functioning."

"What do you usually do in these cases?" said Andy, at a loss.

"Well, doctor," said the charge nurse, "often changing the draining bottle does the trick, but we can't do it without a doctor's authority."

"Please change it," said Andy, "and I'll keep everything crossed until you've done it."

It took about five minutes to change the bottle, and to Andy's relief he saw bloody watery fluid draining in the bottle.

"That's fine," said the charge nurse.

"Thank God," said Andy, "is there anything else I should do?"

"If you could just put a line in his notes," replied the charge nurse and added, "I don't think I've seen you before, sir."

"It's my first night as a doctor," said Andy grinning.

"Who's houseman are you?" said the charge nurse.

"I am Dr Ramsden's HP," said Andy.

"Ah well," said the charge nurse, "you're lucky you have Dr Hudson as your Registrar, he's the best doctor in the hospital, and nice with it."

Dr David Hudson was a nice, small gentleman who always had a little whimsical smile on his face, particularly on ward rounds when he once had to tell Dr Ramsden that he was holding some electrocardiogram reading upside down. David Hudson was reading for his membership and with Andy due to resit the medical part of his degree, made a point of specifically teaching Andy every time some appropriate condition came up.

How good he was became clear when Andy admitted an unconscious man to the ward who had had an epileptic fit. Andy took a careful history from the wife, frequency of fits, et cetera. He learnt that the patient had been investigated at the Neurological Hospital in Queen's Square and they had made a diagnosis of some sort of high brain stem epilepsy. The tablets they had given him were not controlling his fits, which were becoming more frequent and the patient was often violent before a fit then became unconscious, slept for two or three hours, woke up hungry and was then all right until the next fit.

Andy examined the patient and then sent for Dr Hudson.

David Hudson glanced through Andy's notes then asked the wife if she minded answering a few more questions.

"All right," said the wife, a bit reluctantly, "but they did have a go at me at Queen's Square."

"When does your husband have his fits?" said David.

"Any time," said the wife.

"When you said, any time," said David, "are they for example, more often before a meal, or more often after a meal?"

"Now you mention it," said the wife, "it's most often just as we are about to have a meal. I can't tell you how many dinners have spoiled."

"Thank you," said David. "Now if you would like to go and sit in the Day Room and ask Sister if you can have a cup of tea. If she says she would like to, but Matron won't allow it, tell her Dr Hudson has ordered it."

"Now, doctor," said David to Andy, "what do we do now."

"I have no idea," said Andy. "Wait until he comes round I expect."

David said, "Mark this my boy, the golden rule on all unconscious patients. Always do a blood urea, a blood sugar, a lumbar puncture, a blood count, a urine test and a chest X-ray on every patient that is admitted. Often those are the only investigations required. It's surprising what comes up. Have you done a lumbar puncture before?"

"No," said Andy.

"Well, this will be your first," said David.

They began by taking some blood samples and sending them to the laboratory, they then prepared the man as if for an operation. He was laid on his side with head tucked down, knees up. His back was swabbed with iodine then draped with sterile towels, just leaving the lower portion of the back uncovered. David and Andy scrubbed-up and put on sterile caps, gowns, masks and gloves. Sister, similarly dressed, was laying out a lumbar puncture tray with a large pair of forceps, picking-out needles and syringes from a dish filled with some antiseptic fluid, then washing them in a dish of sterile water.

Two chairs were drawn up for Andy and David and they sat facing the exposed back.

"Now," said David, "feel for the third invertebral space."

Andy prodded with his fingers until he found the appropriate spot between two bony spines. Then from the lumbar puncture tray David passed him a three inch hypodermic needle that had a metal plunger in it and a cap. "Now," he said, "gently push this needle into the space you've found, if you hit bone, stop, and come out, if suddenly you are aware that the pressure has no resistance, stop." Andy pushed the needle in tentatively, the skin was tough, it was easier when he got into the softer tissue, then suddenly, no pressure, and he stopped.

"Well you could be first time lucky," said David, "pull out the plunger and see what happens."

Andy pulled out the plunger and a clear, colourless fluid began to drip from the base of the needle.

"Quick, specimen bottle," said David, and a bottle was held under the needle and about ten drops collected.

"Now replace your plunger," said David, "pull out your needle, dig your thumb into the area you shoved the needle in and rub it about, then put some collodium over the injection site — we don't want him to be leaking."

"What do we do now?" asked Andy.

"Well," said David, "what do you think, look at the ward clock, what does that tell you?"

"Oh, it's lunch time," said Andy.

"And," said David, "thereby could hang a tale."

At lunch time David went to the Consultants' table and spoke to Dr Ramsden saying he would like him to see a case in the afternoon. When he rejoined Andy, Andy said, "What does Dr Ramsden do in the afternoons?"

"Sleep mainly," said David, "I didn't want to have to wake him up."

When they got back to the ward the notes from Queen's Square, electro-encephalograph readings et cetera had come over. As David read them his smile became even more whimsical. Having read them he passed them over to Andy. This coincided with results coming up from the Path Lab which David read, then a broad smile crossed his face. "Great," he said, "we're right."

"What d'you mean?" said Andy.

"His blood and Cerebro Spinal Fluid sugars are nil," said David.

"Has he been taking insulin then?" said Andy.

"No," said David, "this almost certainly means that he has an islet cell tumour at the tail of the pancreas. This is a benign tumour which over-secretes insulin, thus our friend here blacks out just when his mouth begins to water at the thought of his dinner. This man is no more epileptic than you or I, all he needs is a small operation to remove this little tumour and our friend here will be all right." They were interrupted by Dr Ramsden. David Hudson had to explain the situation to him as clearly and slowly as he had to Andy. "The proof is in the pudding," said David, "let's give him some intravenous Dextrose."

Sister passed him a large syringe of Dextrose solution.
David injected it into a vein.

In five minutes the patient was fully conscious, asking where he was and demanding food.

"Well done, Hudson," said Dr Ramsden. "I must ring Harry Burgess at Queen's Square and tell him if he wants his patients properly diagnosed he'd better send them over here."

He disappeared into the Sister's Office, Andy and David could only hear snatches of conversation, it was mainly, "I this," and, "I that."

"He's taking all the credit," said Andy, indignantly, "and he didn't do a thing."

"Never mind," said David, "he is a bit dim, but he is the head of our team and, if unlike today, we'd made a mess of something, he would have stood up and taken the flak for us, he's all right."

For the next forty years of Andy's medical life he always had one eye open for an islet cell tumour and was always testing for it, but he never ever saw another case.

The patient was operated on by Diana Reynolds three days later with David and Andy watching. As expected an islet cell tumour was found and easily removed.

Diana Reynolds had an FRCS and was entitled to call herself 'Mr'. She was less like a mister than anyone Andy had ever met. She still completely ignored him as they met on their communal stairway, but there was many a night when Andy massaged himself to sleep with some fantasy about her, but so did many other males in the hospital.

Three months just sped by. It was announced by Mr Farrant that there was to be a Hospital Summer Party for medical staff and their wives only. It was a pretty low-key affair. For once there was plenty to eat and more than plenty to drink. Diana Reynolds had come in a yellow clinging dress that made her look as if she was about to burst from it. By 11 everybody was a bit merry and Mr Farrant called a halt to the proceedings.

Diana and Andy happened to leave at the same time. For the first time ever she spoke to him. "Is your gas ring still working?" she asked Andy.

"Yes," said Andy suddenly alert.

"What can you offer me?" said Diana.

"Cocoa, Ovaltine, tea, coffee," said Andy.

"I'll have some Ovaltine," she said.

"Shall I bring it to you?" said Andy.

"No," she said, "I'll come in with you."

Andy went ahead of her into his room. When Diana came in she had not only locked the door, but bolted it. Suddenly Andy had the biggest erection of his life. He busied himself with the Ovaltine, hardly daring to turn round. Diana prowled around the room and then said casually, "I want to sit on the floor and I can't in this dress, I'll have to take it off." There was a rustling of clothes and Andy's erection nearly hit him on the chin. He made the Ovaltine, turned round with a cup in either hand to find Diana lying on the floor naked, apart from a brief pair of pants, her head reclining on the seat of the armchair. "Come and sit here beside me," she said, patting the floor.

"You know they call you Mouse," said Diana, as Andy came towards her.

"No," said Andy, "why do they call me that?"

"Because you are always scuttling about all over the place."

At that moment Andy had never felt less like a mouse in his life. He handed Diana a cup of Ovaltine then sat down beside her as bidden, hardly being able to believe what was happening.

Diana placed her left hand on Andy's lower abdomen. "My God, whose a big boy," she said.

"Now," she said, "rules of engagement. I am a bit pissed, but if ever you blab about what's going to happen I will ruin you and say you tried to rape me.

"Rule number two, no kissing on the mouth. Number three, practicalities, have you any contraceptives?"

Andy thought, "No," he said. This was probably the first time since he was thirteen that he hadn't carried any.

"Well, it doesn't matter tonight," said Diana, "but get equipped, if you're a good boy you might get some more."

"Is this your first time?" queried Diana.

"Yes," said Andy, blushing.

"Well," she said, "your medical education will be enlarged tonight. Last rule," she said, "everything that happens in this room stops at the door, we don't speak to each other outside. If I want to come to you I will knock five times, now let's get to bed."

She stood up, slipped off her pants and got into bed.

Andy still found it difficult to believe what was happening and went to turn off the light before he undressed.

"Keep the light on," she snapped, then lay on her elbow displaying her beautiful, perfectly shaped breasts, quizzically watching Andy fumbling as he took his clothes off. He walked to the bed very conscious of his erection, then climbed in with her.

She swarmed all over him, just the sensation of her skin contact nearly made him climax. He had barely entered her when he did. They lay together with Diana just fondling his penis, nothing much seemed to happen at first then in a few minutes he was rampant and plunged fully into her, ramming himself home as if he was trying to push her through the bed. Diana groaned, clenching her teeth on a piece of pillow, then with the same sort of good fortune Andy had had with his first lumbar puncture they climaxed together.

Andy felt as if the room was doing somersaults. He lay breathless, still inside her, it was only a few minutes before he started again.

Andy was now in control, it was Diana who broke the kissing rule, or rather the mouth rule. "You can do anything you like to me," said Diana and Andy did.

After a while the confines of the single bed were too limiting so they put the mattress on the floor, covering themselves with a blanket, their sweaty bodies sliding over each other. There was no love or tenderness, no soft word, this was all pure lust, if there is such a thing as pure lust.

Diana cried pax first, she lay back exhausted. "I can't manage any more," she said.

"No, I want you again," he said, mounting her now flaccid body and riding her until they both collapsed exhausted.

Diana could hardly pull her clothes on. "I think I've unleashed a demon," she said, "but don't forget, when I leave this room, that's it, no contact, now put your head outside and see if there's a porter lurking."

Andy looked out as requested and Diana literally dragged herself back to her room.

* * *

She used to appear about twice a week, usually on a Monday and a Thursday, at about 11.30 p.m. There would be five knocks, then she would come in and stay about two hours. There was never the same frenzy as the first night, and once, when Andy started to get emotional and called her "darling" she smacked his face. "It's not like that," she said, "this has all to be on my terms or we pack it in."

She had released a demon in Andy, he could think of nothing but her and her visits. Just to see her sent his blood racing, and he still had to walk past her stony faced. He flung himself into his work during the day.

He wondered where she went to at weekends and what she might be up to. He lay awake restless the nights she didn't come and was exhausted the nights she did come. Weekends off when Diana was away, Andy would go home to his father and Mrs Robinson, who was now 'Auntie Rob'. They noticed a change in him. He would sleep practically all the weekend. "You are overdoing it at the hospital," his father said, little knowing how right he was.

Andy failed his MB medicine, he was just too shagged-out when the exam came round to do himself justice.

David Hudson took him on one side. "Andy," he said, "I don't have to be a brilliant diagnostician to know that there is something wrong, if I can help, ask me."

"No, I'm OK, thanks," said Andy, but they both knew he was lying.

Andy was insanely jealous when he saw Diana talking to any man, but daren't show it. He was 'good old Andy' to the hospital junior staff, as he would volunteer for any work that was going, just to keep himself from going mad. He was the best lumbar puncturing houseman in the hospital, anyone with a difficult one to do called for him to do it.

He had meant to leave the hospital after his House Physician job, but stayed on and did a six-month House Surgeon job. He just could not leave with her about, she physically intoxicated him. Sometimes, when she came, he tried to talk to her, but she always shut him up with, "I haven't come here to talk," so he never got a chance to know her, she deliberately kept him out.

He, of course, failed his degree Medicine the third time.

As his House Surgeon's job was finishing he applied for a mixed job as a Senior House Officer in eyes, skin, ENTs, orthopaedics, plastics and venereal diseases. Nobody had applied for this job before in living memory, it had just been filled for the occasional month by the odd locum, it was an impossible job, but it would keep Andy at the hospital near Diana.

He began to hate Diana. He made up his mind that the next time she came he would send her away, but, of course, he never did. Then she didn't appear for a week and he nearly went crazy. He almost went up to her in the hospital, but her eyes blazed at him and it cut him short.

In the last week of his House Surgeon's job, while assisting at an operation, the Surgeon, Mr Farrant said, "Have you got an invitation to the Dinner tonight, Andy?"

Andy, out of touch with all social events, said, "Which Dinner?"

"You know," said Mr Farrant, "it's our Diana and her fiancé's goodbye dinner before they fly out to Australia on Friday."

Andy almost let go of the retractor he was holding, the room seemed to spin round. "Who is her fiancé?" he eventually asked.

"You know," said Mr Farrant, "that banker chap, he's not quite a Rothschild but something of that ilk."

Mr Farrant wouldn't shut up about the Dinner. It was in the main hospital restaurant, there was outside catering, and black tie. Was Andy sure he hadn't been invited?

"I remember now," said Andy lying in his teeth, "I had to cancel, my father is ill."

"Pity," said Mr Farrant.

Fortunately this was the last operation of the day. Somehow Andy managed to get the patient back to the ward and he got back to his room and lay on his bed. He was in pain, he groaned, he just couldn't believe it, the bitch, the whore, he could kill her, yes, he really could kill her. He was almost out of his mind, he lay on his bed staring at the ceiling.

He must have lain there for about three hours, the room was in complete darkness. He was startled by his bedside telephone ringing.

"Are you in?" said a whispered voice that could have been the

Casualty Sister.

"Of course I'm in," snarled Andy, "otherwise I wouldn't have answered."

"Could you come to Casualty?" said the whispered voice in a sob, "there's a man down here with a knife at Staff Nurse's throat, please come."

Andy was off his bed and down the stairs in a flash. He ran along the corridor to Casualty, snatching up a piece of lead piping from a pile of building material lying in the corridor as he ran. He burst through the Casualty doors and, as a coloured man in the room, a stiletto knife to the Staff Nurse's throat, turned, startled, Andy smashed the pipe at his arm breaking it and sending the knife flying. He went in again with the pipe, and smashed the man on the arm again to make sure. As he did so he was conscious, from the corner of his eye of a man coming up off a couch at him from the right, so he ducked and swung the pipe outwards, smashing the man in the face. As he ducked he felt a searing pain across the top of his scalp and blood began to pour down his face. He turned, and there was a third man with a type of short bayonet knife. As Andy turned he must have looked a fearful sight. He was snarling, blood pouring down his face. The man began to back off, Andy was suddenly cool. He walked towards the man slowly. "I'm going to have you, you bastard," said Andy. Andy was conscious of nurses screaming, and police sirens in the distance.

The man ran into Out Patients. Andy went in behind him, bolted the main door then went towards the cubicles where he knew the man must be hiding. He kicked in each cubicle door methodically until he found one that wouldn't open. He then began to smash the plywood door with his lead pipe. The man inside was screaming in terror. As Andy was smashing through he heard a noise behind him, and suddenly there was a police sergeant either side of him holding his arms. "Steady son," said one, "we will take over now."

There were police swarming all over the place. The two sergeants led Andy away, one of them taking the lead pipe. They took him to a curtained off part in Casualty. As he went in he noticed the two other men he had hit were still on the floor, both with police and nurses in attendance.

He lay down on the couch. There was so much blood coming

down his face that he could hardly see. He could just make out the startled face of a dinner-jacketed Mr Farrant appear.

"You lost your temper a bit," said one of the sergeants.

"Yes," said Andy, "I hope I haven't hurt them too much." He was suddenly cool, as if all the hate had been washed out of him.

"Don't worry," said the sergeant, "you couldn't have hurt that lot enough, you've done our work for us, we've been after these three for a long time, they're pimps, illegal immigrants and as soon as they are patched up, they'll be off to Germany."

"They don't look German," said Andy.

"They're not," said the sergeant, "I don't know their country of origin, but they came to England from Germany."

"Is there anybody you'd like to see?" said the sergeant.

"Yes," said Andy, "O'Sullivan."

"I'm here, man," said O'Sullivan, who had obviously been listening all the time. The sergeants left and O'Sullivan came in, "Jesus," he said, looking at the bloody Andy, "I'm sure glad you're on our side. I came from home. I thought war had broken out." He massaged Andy's shoulders, "Dr Reynolds tried to get in to see you, I told her, 'No, man'."

It dawned on Andy that there was nothing that went on in the hospital that O'Sullivan didn't know about. "By the way," said O'Sullivan, "you owe me a bottle of whisky."

"I'll make it two," said Andy.

They cleaned Andy up. His injury was no more than a scalp wound, it was cleaned, sutured and they put him in an Observation Ward for the night, then sent him home on two weeks' leave.

CHAPTER 7

ON THE TREADMILL

When Andy arrived home on leave, there was some explaining to do as he did not think that Auntie Rob and his father believed that he had just been attacked in Casualty. Fortunately, the incident did not get into the papers. At the time, in some areas near the hospital, there had been what had become known as 'an accommodation war' going on. Either blacks or whites would buy, say, the remaining five years of a lease for an apartment in one of the big broken-down houses. They would then create so much trouble for the rest of the tenants in the house, that this would drive them out and they would then fill the whole building with relatives and friends, which could easily add up to about a hundred people. It could be blacks doing this to whites or whites against blacks, blacks against blacks, or whites against whites. These mini riots occurred frequently, and the presence of so many police in Casualty was due to the fact that one of these riots had just been cleared up a couple of streets away from the hospital, when the call for help had come from Casualty.

The nurses in Casualty were so bemused by all the action that no one person had seen all Andy's actions. With him out of the way, and fresh dramas occurring almost nightly, what he did, was largely forgotten, although, until he left the hospital, there was always a vague story that he'd been a hero and was somebody not to meddle with.

For Andy the incident was a blessing. It purged him of all his pent up feeling about Diana. He wasn't sure if the last nine months had been taken from a romantic novel, certainly the last bit was *Boys' Own*. He no longer blamed her, she had made the situation clear from the beginning and he, of course, could always have said 'no'. For the first time he had seen the power of physical relationships and the cost.

On his second day at home, two policemen called to see him. Did he want to press charges? "No," said Andy.

"Good," said the police, "that saves us a lot of paper work, and this lot will be out of the country in two weeks. None of them know who you are, they think you are the wild man from Borneo, you certainly looked a bit frightening. It's surprising that a cut on your head caused so much blood."

"It only takes the smallest of scalp wounds," said Andy, "to make you look as if you've been mauled by a tiger."

"How did you know how to tackle things?" said one of the police.

"Well, as a boy," said Andy, "I always used to read the *Hotspur*, and there was a white man with a cricket bat and his native companion with two knives. One, or both of them, was called 'Clicky Bar' and the two of them would take on a hundred tribesmen at a time, and they never ever lost. I could really have done with a cricket bat."

The policemen laughed, "Well sir, if you ever feel like joining the force we would be pleased to have you on our side, and we could guarantee you a cricket bat."

After five days at home the time began to drag a bit and Auntie Rob and his father, who was almost retired, just doing the occasional consulting work, had just about used up all possible conversation, when Auntie Rob timidly suggested that her cottage in Instow in North Devon was not booked for a week or two and they were welcome to it.

Auntie Rob's cottage at Instow had been in her family for years. She was the last of the family, and for a long time had been going to sell it, then always, at the last minute, she changed her mind. She hadn't seen it for years, but the cottage was full of memories of her childhood. She had had a honeymoon there, and thought, suppose somebody nasty bought it and knocked it about. So each year she put it off and put it back in the hands of the agents for letting.

Andy and his father jumped at the idea. In the middle of their packing, Andy had the thought. "Dad," he said, "do you think we ought to ask Auntie Rob if she'd like to come down with us?"

"We could ask her," said his father, "I can't remember when she last went away."

His father went round to see her and was back in five minutes. He said it was like breaking the news to someone that they'd won the pools. She was quite overcome. She was like a schoolgirl in her excitement, and, he said, with his face lighting up, "We won't have to cook."

The cottage at Instow was a simple plain brick building with three bedrooms, kitchen, bathroom, lounge/dining-room and a small garden, with a garage at the back, but heaven, the lounge/dining-room opened onto a covered patio that faced the river estuary with Appledore on the other side. Without unpacking, Andy sank into a deck chair — this was peace. There were boats coming up and down the river, a large gravel digger, small boats with only one man in each who had gone down-river with the tide. Using a shovel, each filled his boat with a ton of gravel or sand and were now coming back up-river with the tide. There was a Scandinavian timber boat on its way up to Bideford, and just to spoil things, a landing craft from the Army Vehicle Waterproofing Station further down at Instow.

Instow is on the banks of the River Torridge. About a mile past the cottage, the Torridge meets the River Taw coming from Barnstaple, emptying into what is known as Bideford Bay if you live in Bideford, or Barnstaple Bay if you live in Barnstaple. The sun shone, and all was right with the world.

His father and Auntie Rob went off each day in the car and she showed him all the places she'd known in her younger days, Ilfracombe, Lynton, Lynmouth, Combe Martin, Woolacombe, Croyde Bay, Westward Ho! and Bideford.

It was enough for Andy to sit and watch the world go by. There was always something happening in the estuary, and for the first time he saw salmon seine-net fishing. Two men rowed out with one end of a net, whilst the other end was anchored on shore. The boat would do a circle to reach its fixed end, then, with about three men on each side, the net was dragged up the beach with flashes of silver as the fish were landed. Andy watched it all with binoculars, and wondered how long such a large volume of salmon would keep coming up the Torridge at the rate they were taking them out.

Most lunch times, by really summoning up all his strength, he managed to get down the road to the Marine Hotel for a pint of beer and a sandwich. They all loathed the thought of going back.

Two days before they were due to go, Andy went into Bideford and saw a friendly Dr Wake, who removed his stitches, Andy telling him how he had acquired his injury.

"Well," said Dr Wake, with a twinkle in his eye as he took an off-work certificate out of a drawer, "another week down here would do you no harm young man."

Andy was delighted, but he wondered how the others would feel.

"That's marvellous," squealed Auntie Rob, "I still want to show your father Clovelly and the Glass Works at Torrington — the cottage is free."

His father looked at them both and smiled and said, "Only a week, I could stay here for a year."

After supper Andy went down to the Marine Hotel and bought a bottle of sparkling wine which was the nearest to champagne he could afford. He came solemnly into the cottage, made the others sit down at the table with a glass in front of them, poured them a glass of sparkling wine and said, "I have an official announcement to make. "Auntie Rob, up to now, you have just been Auntie Rob from next door, from this night on and for evermore, you are our official, adopted aunt, and are now Auntie Rob proper. Let's raise our glasses and drink to it." Auntie Rob put her glass down, then, with a handkerchief clasped to her face, rushed off to her bedroom in tears. "Gosh dad, what have I done?" said Andy, "this is awful."

His father laughed, "Don't you know, son, that women only cry when they are happy, you have made her the happiest woman in the West of England."

The second week went all too quickly. Andy was fitter than he had been for a year. He had this dreadful mixed job to face when he got back, but in a way, it was a challenge. He was anxious to get back to medicine where he could work without the strain of his relationship with Diana.

It was time to go back to the hospital.

"Is there anything I can get you before you go?" said Andy's father.

Andy paused for a moment and then said, "There is something if you can, it's expensive, and it's for a debt and no questions asked please."

"Come on," said his father, "what is it, the Forth Bridge?"

"No," said Andy, "two bottles of whisky."

His father was just about to comment, checked himself, reached into his wallet and pulled out some notes. "Now," he said, "go on, up to the off-licence, I hope you're not a secret drinker."

His father drove him back to St Daniel's, and as the building came in sight Andy thought back to his last night there. How far would he have gone if he'd been able to break into the Out Patient cubicle before the police reached him, he would never know.

His room looked dingy and drab as ever and his heart sank a bit, but several of the other Housemen popped in to say hello. There was quite a gathering at 9 o'clock for cocoa and lots of gossip, with everybody wanting to know exactly what had happened. Andy brushed them off by putting their questions back to them, and asking what had happened in the hospital while he'd been away.

Over the next few days Andy tried to sort out this new complicated job. He met the larger than life Mr Gotter, the orthopaedic surgeon. He had asked Mr Farrant's opinion of him and Mr Farrant had said, smiling, "Well, the rest of the staff think he's a refugee from a Cronin novel."

Mr Gotter, overwhelmed by the fact that at last he'd got a Senior House Officer, said, "Don't forget I'll take up most of your time."

As they were speaking, a drug house representative, who seemed to have twisted his neck, came up to see the surgeon.

"Ah," said Mr Gotter, "what's the matter?"

"Oh, my neck's a bit stiff," said the rep, and there in the middle of the corridor, in spite of the chap's protests, Mr Gotter manipulated him.

Mr Gotter was hated by the staff, although he was a hard worker. Andy could never make up his mind whether he was a good surgeon or not. Some things he did well, others he didn't. He never ever wrote a letter to a doctor about the patients he'd treated, and he never answered a letter written to him. Andy forlornly tried to get some sort of correspondence going, but as he had several other masters, it was impossible.

He approached the dermatologist, another of his consultants, who said he would always be welcomed at the clinic, but if he didn't know anything about skins, he wasn't much use to him.

He made the mistake of going to the venereal disease ward to meet the VD consultant. What he hadn't appreciated was that the VD part of his job was solely confined to young ladies who were convicts from Holloway Prison who had some form of this disease. He walked boldly into the ward and then ran for safety to the Sister's office as a dozen girls leapt from their beds to shout, "Look girls, a man."

The lady venereologist came in and lifted the siege. She said, "It's amazing, it's the first time that my so-called Senior House Officer has ever appeared, but I'm happy to tell you I don't need you. I'll escort you to the door so that you are not assaulted."

The eye consultant was an extremely nice man, Mr Seal, who said, "You have an impossible job, Andy, but if you've come to me, and if you're going into general practice, there are a few minor operations that I can teach you that will be very useful to you when you do get into general practice, as these are all done under local anaesthetic."

The consultant he liked best was Dr Nuberg, the ear nose and throat consultant. "It's great to have some help," he said to Andy, "and I'll be happy to teach you all you want to know."

Dr Nuberg was not the only person who did ear nose and throat surgery at the hospital. Various people came in and did tonsillectomy lists and dashed out again, and Andy had this continuing nightmare of children having post-operative tonsil bleeding. The man who always made himself available, and would come in, regardless of whose case it was, was Dr Nuberg. He made a point of teaching Andy whenever Andy could get to his clinics, looking down ears, up noses, down throats and in the theatre he was training him to take out tonsils.

The plastic surgeons were extremely high powered. A very large, pompous man, with a famous name, from Guys, and another man, a bit of a wag, who came from East Grinstead, was his assistant. What they were doing at St Daniel's Hospital Andy had no idea. All sorts of people used to turn up, and he was pretty sure they were seeing some private patients there and treating them.

He remembered one day when Maxwell, the junior of the two was holding an Out Patients. In came a very well known actress to say she thought there was something wrong with her breast reduction operation. "Let's have a look," said Dr Maxwell. This beautiful young woman took off her blouse and bra and the sight beneath was appalling. There were great scars on her breast, her right nipple was pointing towards her right arm and the left breast looked a bit tatty, but was far better than the right. "That's an absolutely fine, successful operation," said Dr Maxwell, "we will have to do a bit more work, but I'm sure Mr Clarke will be delighted to hear how you are getting on when I tell him."

When she'd gone Andy said, "Excuse me sir, am I losing my reason? I thought that looked like a disaster."

"You're absolutely right," said Dr Maxwell, "I daren't tell the girl that. You see, the trouble is, with any breast reduction, you never quite know how it's going to finish up. What you can't estimate is how much fat absorption there will be, and however good it looks, at the end of the operation, you keep your fingers crossed. Clarke is the expert on putting things right, and this girl will be all right, but she'll need another op."

The case under them that was incredible and made Andy forgive them, whatever they were doing privately, was a patient called Edna Clarence, who had had cancer of the larynx which meant her larynx had been removed completely. She had a hole under her chin where saliva dripped, there was a tube going into her lungs and another into her stomach to feed her and there was a space between the chin and the top of her chest. These two plastic surgeons were patiently building an artificial larynx for her, so that in time she would be able to take food by mouth. This needed incredible skill and this lady, who was always cheerful and became a great favourite of Andy's, would be in a hospital for at least two years.

So, as usual, Andy was on the run from the orthopaedics to the plastics, to the ENTs, only occasionally getting into eyes, hardly ever getting into the skins, and fortunately leaving the venereal diseases alone.

He was the oldest resident now. It was always important to him to be thought well of by everybody, and he went out of his way to be a sort of father figure to people starting their first jobs. He was at everybody's beck and call, showing people for the first time how to cross-match blood. He had been strictly told, by Mr Farrant, that he must not go into Casualty, but it didn't stop him going in occasionally with a mask on his face to help when they were very pressed.

The hospital was beginning to look in rather better shape now. They were spending money on decorating and doing up wards and theatres, and there was some talk of it being added as a sort of secondary teaching place to St Jane's Hospital where Andy had trained, but it needed a huge face-lift before that would be possible. Andy thought, 'My God, fancy Mr Gotter lecturing to medical students.'

His job really was just too much for him. He had an Army medical pending before doing his National Service, and although it would be deferred to the end of this job, he wondered whether the Army might say they wanted him straight away. He hoped so. He fancied himself in a Sam Brown belt and an officer's uniform. He might be sent abroad, or all sorts of exciting things could happen.

He duly received a call-up notice for his medical and went off to it cheerfully. He did the usual things, coughed at the right time and had a physician listen to his chest. He listened a bit too long Andy thought, had a chest X-ray, urine test and blood tests. Andy came back from his medical, cheered. It did mean there was an end in sight to this present tremendous grind, where he was rushing from pillar to post, getting patients ready for theatre, pre-medication, then seeing them post-operatively. He even toyed with the idea of becoming a permanent Army Medical Officer and making the Army his career. Anyway he was really looking forward to his two years.

To his huge disappointment a brown official looking letter written on Her Majesty's Service arrived. On opening it he read, not believing what he saw that following the medical examination at, and then it went on to list the building and address, 'We are sorry to report that Dr Andrew Howard has not passed as being medically fit to take up service in Her Majesty's Forces.'

He went to David Hudson and showed him the letter. "Right," said David, "we'll give you the complete works." David went over him from toe-nails to eyebrows, with blood test, chest X-rays, everything. They sat down together when the results came in. "Andy," said David, "you're absolutely 100% fit, you have a slight systolic murmur, but it is purely physiological and of no significance." With a letter from David he went to see a Harley Street Consultant who confirmed everything that David said. He then wrote to the Army with a letter from David and from the Harley Street specialist, but the Army wouldn't budge. There was to be no military service for Andy.

"I just don't understand it," said Andy to David, "I'm probably the fittest Houseman in London."

"Yes," said David, "and I know how good a doctor you are, and I know qualifications don't really mean a thing, but to date you only have LMSSA and to some, stupidly, that matters."

Fortunately Andy's work kept him so busy that whatever disappointment he had was soon replaced by exhaustion. Everybody else was talking about what they were going to do in their military service, and where they hoped to go. He just kept quiet. Once again he was going to be an outsider. He wanted to get into general practice, but he still had months of this terrible job to do and he would have to do an obstetric job somewhere before he could even start thinking of applying for a job in general practice.

David Hudson tried to comfort him. He said, "It's strange, Andy, half the people here would give their eye teeth not to have to go in the Army and you're fretting because you can't."

"I," he said, "believe that somehow there is an overall pattern to our lives, and remember, this, my boy, could be part of your pattern.

Perhaps something good will turn up you'd have missed if you'd gone into the Army."

"Well, if something good does turn up," said Andy, "it'll have to be very good."

He then shot off once more on to the treadmill of work that this strange mixed job demanded.

CHAPTER 8

FULLY ENGAGED

Andy was on the children's ward examining little Amy aged four years who had a bone tumour on her leg. A biopsy had shown it to be malignant, but it was a low grade malignancy and there was a chance that it could be operated on successfully, but she had to have some chemotherapy and radiotherapy first.

She had been on the ward for about a month now, and he wished that it could be someone other than Mr Gotter who was eventually going to operate on her. He had to take some blood from her, which he hated. He played with her for a while, bopping her on the nose with a toy rabbit, then went into the pathology room of the ward to get the syringes and specimen bottles. He mused, and wondered if Dr Nuberg really meant it when he said unless Andy brought somebody to the hospital ball he wouldn't let him take out another tonsil. "You're all work and no play, Andy," he said, "it makes for a dull boy."

Since the departure of Diana, Andy had kept his head down and worked with only the occasional visit home. Having cut out both skins and venereal disease parts of his job, it was still an impossible one.

He had told the Ward Sister he would need a nurse to help with the blood. He nodded to the Sister as he walked back towards the screened-off Amy. At the same time he noticed the door opening and Matron and her entourage sweeping in.

As he went through the curtains Amy began to cry when she saw the bottles and syringes. "Oh, don't cry," said Andy, "Dr Andy doesn't want to hurt you. I know, we'll take blood from teddy first," then he went through an elaborate charade of pretending to take blood from teddy, wishing that a nurse would come and they could get it all finished.

No nurse came, but Andy could hear Matron in a loud booming voice slanging some nurse off and sounding like a sergeant major. Andy felt one of his energy surges coming on, he thought there must be some violent side to his nature, he could easily go and hit Matron with a lead pipe.

In a couple of minutes he was at boiling point.

He stormed out from Amy's curtained-off bed, then pointing his finger at Matron he said in a very loud voice, "Matron just shut up, this is a hospital, not a barrack room, and you, nurse," pointing to the one who was getting slagged-off, "come and help me with this child."

There was a deadly silence, the slim fair-haired nurse looked at Matron and Andy, not quite knowing what to do.

"Come on nurse," said Andy, kindly, "we're running a hospital, and I need your help."

As the nurse came to help him, Matron led her retinue out of the ward. The rather red-eyed nurse was a natural, she cuddled Amy, Andy took her blood with just one little yelp from Amy. "Was that teddy talking?" he asked, then he took his blood to the path room and set up some tests.

He had been in there about ten minutes when there was a knock on the door. "Come in," said Andy. In came the nurse who had been helping him, "Yes," said Andy.

"I just wanted to thank you, sir," said the nurse.

"Thank me," said Andy, "what for?"

"For rescuing me from Matron," said the nurse, "you are my knight in shining armour."

"No, I'm not," said Andy, "it's just the starch in these white coasts. What dreadful crime did you commit, and will she get at you when I'm not here."

"No," said the nurse, "they're all slightly scared of you, didn't you once knock somebody about in Casualty or something? My crime was to drop and break a china bed pan, there aren't many of them about nowadays. Anyway, thanks. If there's anything I can ever do for you I would."

Andy cut her short, "As a matter of fact you can come along as my partner to the hospital ball."

"Why me?" said the girl.

"Well, you asked," said Andy, "and I've been ordered to go."

"Well, I haven't a long dress," said the nurse, "I've never been to a ball before."

"Never mind," said Andy, "you have until ten to seven Friday week to make, beg, borrow or steal one."

"I don't know," said the nurse.

"Right," said Andy, "I'll send for Matron."

The nurse smiled, "All right, I'll do my best, sir."

"By the way," said Andy as she was leaving, "what's your name?"

"Mary Smith, sir," said the girl.

"Well, that stands out in a crowd," said Andy, "and I'm Andy, not sir."

"Oh, I couldn't sir," said the girl.

"Say Andy," said Andy.

"Andy," said the girl, and giggled.

"Ten to seven Friday week it will be," said Andy.

She was a trim, neat, poised little nurse. 'I could have done worse,' thought Andy.

He scrubbed up that afternoon with Dr Nuberg for the tonsil list. As they stood at adjoining sinks Andy said, "Mary Smith."

"Whose Mary Smith?" said Dr Nuberg.

"My partner for the ball," said Andy.

"I don't believe you," said Dr Nuberg, "and you could have thought of a more original name."

"Mary Smith is a nurse on the children's ward who I saved from Matron's wrath today."

"OK, a bargain's a bargain," said Dr Nuberg, and he carefully supervised while Andy took out four lots of tonsils.

The next few days after his tonsillectomies Andy's time was fully occupied by the plastic surgeons, who were for once proving their mettle. It was the second stage in the rebuilding of Edna Clarence's larynx, and for the first time Andy was able to see what patient and skilled men they were. It meant that for the following two days his time was taken up purely looking after her, and both the ear nose and throat, orthopaedic and eye areas of his work had to suffer. In the past all the consultants had taken this for norm, they weren't used to having anybody around, but having had Andy for six months, there were a few grumbles, but you just can't please all the people all the time, and Andy has to select his priorities.

The following week on the orthopaedic list Mr Gotter was almost lynched by the surgery staff. He was doing a halux vulgus toe operation on a retired nurse. He'd done one foot, made the incision on another then said, "I haven't time to finish it today, I've got another patient to go and see," and to the fury of the theatre staff, stitched the foot up and sent the patient back to the ward.

"Come on Andy," he said, "I need your help."

Andy climbed into his Rolls-Royce with him, and they shot off to some private nursing home where the theatre staff were all geared up waiting for him.

The anaesthetist had the patient on a trolley lying face downwards and they wheeled her into theatre.

"What are we doing?" said Andy.

"Oh," said Mr Gotter, "we're chopping a bit of her sacrum out."

"Why are we doing that?" said Andy.

"Well," said Mr Gotter, "this poor woman's husband died of a coronary in the middle of the marital act. She's had a back pain ever since and a little operation will take her mind off it."

Andy said nothing, no wonder his colleagues called Mr Gotter "a refugee from a Cronin novel."

He had to slip home one night and pick up his father's dinner jacket, he knew it fitted him as he'd borrowed it before, but not for a year or two. This sent Auntie Rob into squeals of excitement. "Have you got a young lady, Andy," she said.

"No," said Andy, "I just have to take somebody to the ball."

They found a proper shirt for him with a black tie and he rushed back to the hospital fully equipped.

The rest of the week was fairly mundane, ward rounds, out patients, nothing dramatic and not too much disturbed sleep. He was called down to Casualty late Friday afternoon to give a hand with a patient, and it was a bit of a rush getting dressed for the evening ball. He noticed as he left his room it was five to seven. 'Oh God,' he thought, 'five minutes late already.'

Happily, when he got to the Nurses' Home, the only person

waiting outside was a slim, elegant, fair-haired girl dressed in a red taffeta dress and a white stole. He looked around for Mary, wondering whether he would recognize her. The girl in the taffeta dress was making questioning eyes at him. This went on for a minute or two as Andy paced up and down. Suddenly the girl walked towards him and said, "You were serious about tonight, sir?"

"Are you Mary Smith?" said Andy incredulously, "you're just gorgeous."

"Oh don't say that, sir," said Mary, "I'm all of a twitter."

"On one condition," said Andy.

"Any condition," said Mary.

"That you call me Andy, and not sir."

"Oh dear," said Mary, "all right, Andy."

"Take my arm," said Andy, "and off we go."

The ball was very pleasant and Mary was a good, unobtrusive companion. Andy had to desert her from time to time and she sat demurely in the background. He noticed that one or two people asked her to dance, but she politely refused. Mr Nuberg insisted on being introduced to her. "Are you really Mary Smith?" he said.

"Yes, sir," she said.

"Well," he said, "you're dancing with the chap who could take your tonsils out if you wanted."

"What does all that mean?" asked Mary.

"Oh, it's a long story," said Andy, "only a bit of fun."

He did find it difficult to take his eyes off her. She was pretty, short, fair haired, freckled — lovely freckled arms — with a slim figure, elegance and poise, a real credit to him. God, how lucky he'd been with his choice. As they danced past Matron and her cronies they saw them nodding with knowing looks, as much as to say 'So that's why he came out shouting down the ward.'

Mary was a good dancer, very light on her feet and the evening rushed by all too quickly. For some reason at the end they sang Auld Lang Syne, although New Year was a good six weeks off and Andy took Mary back to the Nurses' Home. "Thank you so much, sir."

"It's Andy," he said.

"I can go back to calling you sir now," she said, "I feel like Cinderella and I have so enjoyed myself, you'll never know how much." She leaned forward and pecked Andy on the cheek and fled into the Nurses' Home. He was vaguely aware of about eight other faces pressed to various windows watching their goodbye.

This evening off from work had in some way unsettled Andy, and although he worked as hard as ever, he did feel that perhaps it wouldn't be too bad to do something social occasionally, but how and who to go with and what? He had just got out of the habit.

A month after the ball, walking along the main corridor, he bumped into Mary and impulsively said, "Do you fancy tea and the flicks?"

"I'd love to," she said, "Andy," and smiled.

"When are you next off?"

"Saturday," said Mary.

"Fine," said Andy, "I know a place in Chelsea where we can see foreign films and a café across the road where they do either fish teas or fish suppers."

They were good easy companions, not really intruding into each other's lives, and once a fortnight it became a habit to go to the pictures and have something to eat in Chelsea. Andy always insisted on paying, but Mary was always trying to pay her whack.

Christmas came and went, and with all the hullabaloo there is on wards at Christmas Andy did not see much of Mary.

He felt awful when, on Christmas Day, he found a little parcel outside his room. He unwrapped it and found a nice tie and a note, 'Love from Mary,' and he hadn't got her anything!

Soon after Christmas, every other Saturday, they started their pictures and tea or supper again, until, one Saturday, Mary apologized and said she wouldn't be able to go with him as she had another commitment.

Andy felt completely mortified. She gave no reason for this. 'Bloody women,' he thought, but then, back in his room, he mulled it over and wondered whether she was trying it on. Was she trying to make me jealous? but of course not, theirs was just a sort of brother/sister relationship. Just companionship, she had every reason to go out. He'd forget her. He always had work to fall back on and he blotted her out and worked even harder than usual.

One Friday night there was a knock at the door. He opened it to find Mary — she was blushing.

"Forward of me," she said, "but I would love to go to the

pictures tomorrow."

"Come in you idiot," he said, "and have a cup of cocoa."

"We are not allowed in the doctors' rooms, sir."

"Well, we'll risk it," said Andy.

They went to the pictures first this time, and then went to their little restaurant for their plaice, chips and salad supper. Neither of them had much money. Andy was curious as to where she had been. "You never say anything about your family," he said, "I often speak of mine."

There was a pause. Mary said, "I have no family, I'm a genuine orphan."

"Oh, I'm sorry," said Andy, and for the first time since he'd known her he saw her really tighten up.

"There's absolutely nothing to be sorry about," she said, "I had the happiest childhood imaginable and I missed the other weekend because it was the Silver Wedding of the Master and the Mother of my Home, I couldn't have had a happier time there, I haven't a normal family, but I have a much much bigger one outside." As she said this her eyes became moist. This took the whole edge off the evening, and conversation was a bit stilted.

Andy thought, 'You stupid jealous fool, you've ruined everything.'

They caught the bus back to the stop near the hospital. As they were walking to the hospital, for the first time Mary slipped her hand in his and squeezed it. Holding hands, both clasping tightly, meant much more than either of them could have said with words. He saw her to the door and pecked her on the cheek.

Three days later was the eventful day of little Amy's operation. The radiotherapy and chemotherapy had not gone as well as expected, but there was still hope with this operation. Mary had come with her from the ward, and smiled at Andy in the anaesthetic room. She stayed in theatre, robed, while the operation was performed. Mr Gotter, was his usual loud flamboyant self, flinging instruments about. It was a difficult operation, sometimes he could do things well, but when the leg was fully opened, things did look a bit dicey. They had been operating for about two hours when the anaesthetist said, "Hold on, there is something going wrong, we're losing her."

Then there was about half an hour of frantic resuscitation. The anaesthetist, who was very good, did everything. Adrenalin was put into her heart, but the poor little thing had died.

Andy could think of no apparent reason. One minute all was going well and everything was pink, but the next thing her blood lost colour and she was gone. It couldn't have been her heart, he was just lost.

Mr Gotter took command. "Right," he said, "we just have to carry on and finish the list then we're all going for a drink."

"What about the parents?" said Andy, "they're waiting in the ward day-room."

"Well, you'd better go off and see them," said Mr Gotter.

"I'll go with him," said Mary.

'Oh Christ,' thought Andy as he disrobed, 'what am I going to do?' Mary was taking her theatre stuff off as well, neither of them speaking.

As they walked back down the corridor to the ward, he suddenly felt his arm being squeezed encouragingly. He went to the parents with Mary, it was a tremendous comfort having her with him, and he told them, "I have the most awful news for you, little Amy hasn't made it, she died on the operating table."

The parents, who had been so full of hope in the morning, were now completely distraught, although Andy and Mary comforted them as best they could, and Sister came in with cups of tea.

When they had got over the first shock of their grief the father said, "We would like to see Mr Gotter."

Andy's heart sank. "Well, I'm afraid you can't until he's finished his operating list," said Andy.

"Never mind, we'll wait," said Amy's father. Mary stayed with them while Andy went back to the theatre and stayed until the list was finished, which took about another two hours.

He said to Mr Gotter, "the parents want to see you sir, they'll wait until the list's over."

"Hmm," said Mr Gotter, and no more.

At the end of the list, without speaking, Mr Gotter got rid of his gown, mask, theatre pyjamas and boots, and attended by Andy, walked out to see Amy's parents. Andy wondered what was going to happen. They went into the day-room and both parents got up, "Mr

Gotter," said the father, "we felt we couldn't leave without thanking you for all you did for our Amy. Thank you sir."

"I'm sorry it ended as it did," said Mr Gotter, "I'm afraid I can't tell you what happened, but alas her outlook was very poor anyway, but we did lose the chance we had." He made a hurried exit, shooed Sister out of the office and appeared to be poring over some papers, but, as Andy passed the office, he looked closely and could see this bluff, loud, apparently heartless man, weeping. What a dreadful day.

He wearily did whatever ward work he had, returning to the children's ward to write up some notes. Mary was still there.

"Oh excuse me sir, could I see you in the pathology room please?"

'Oh God,' thought Andy, 'what's this?' "All right nurse," he said. They walked into the pathology room. "What is it Mary," he said patiently.

"Andy, my dear," she said, "I just had to come and give you a big hug," and she buried her head in his shoulder and they clung to each other.

After a sleepless night in bed, Andy was all action, rushing to see his Bank Manager one lunch time, and to a jeweller another. They were due to go for their usual pictures and meal the next Saturday.

Saturday came, and they went to the pictures to see an early programme, planning to eat afterwards. They sat in the restaurant after the film and, whilst waiting to be served, Andy said to Mary, "I think I have an answer to your problem of a lack of family."

"I'm not quite with you," said Mary.

"I think I have it here," said Andy, and from his pocket he produced a small wrapped box.

"You mean there's a family in there," said Mary, smiling.

"It could be," said Andy.

Mary took off the paper, and when she saw the box was from a jeweller she began to blush. When she opened it and saw a ring, "Oh this is lovely, Andy," she said, "I've no jewellery," and began to put it on a finger of her right hand.

"Whoa," said Andy, "give it me," and he put it on the third finger of her left hand.

Mary looked startled.

"Calm down," said Andy, "you're just the nicest person that I've ever know, I love you and I want to marry you."

"You mean that, Andy," said Mary, "you hardly know me."

"Mary, my love," he said, "I know all I want to know about you."

Mary said, "One day when I was at the Home and had been unwell the mother at the Home said, 'Never mind Mary, one day your knight in shining armour will come along and ride away with you to his castle.' Oh Andy, darling, are you sure?"

"I have never been more sure of anything in my life," said Andy, "the remaining question is, will you have me?"

"Of course I will," she said, "I've loved you since the day you saved me from Matron."

"We will make a special date," said Andy, "and we'll go and meet your father-in-law to be and a real live auntie."

Mary said, "I never thought that life could be as good as this."

They walked back to the hospital arm in arm. "Well Mrs Howard-to-be," he said, "bollocks to everybody, you're coming up for a cup of cocoa."

They had hardly sat down when there was a knock at the door. 'Oh God, who's this?' thought Andy, 'we don't want bother tonight.'

It was O'Sullivan.

"Man," said O'Sullivan, waving a bottle of rum, "I have come to congratulate the happy couple."

"How on earth did you know?" asked Andy, "I only proposed an hour ago."

"There's nothing that goes on in this hospital that I don't know about," said O'Sullivan. "Now, quick, drink up, I want to be home and tell the missus."

CHAPTER 9

THE GODS SHONE

Andy had to go to little Amy's post-mortem, he hated these with all their indignities. He just had to steel himself. Happily now, he had Mary. He could always think of her, though he couldn't forget that he had been playing with this lovely little girl just a few days before.

The result of the post-mortem was that the death had been caused by a fat embolism. This gave some relief as there was no way of avoiding it, and it was nobody's fault or due to any negligence. The great post operative killer is the pulmonary embolism where a clot from the leg goes to the heart and lungs causing death. In this case some fatty bone marrow from the leg had done the same thing. Although Andy had heard of it he had never seen it and it meant Amy couldn't have been unluckier, poor little scrap.

Andy rang Mr Gotter to tell him the news. "Just what I thought," said Mr Gotter. He and Andy weren't on good terms nowadays, as Andy refused to leave the hospital to assist in his private work.

'You lying bugger,' thought Andy.

Life, generally, was mad. He just wanted to see Mary all the time and was always popping down to the children's ward just to be able to look at her. She came to his room each evening when she was off duty, always having changed out of her uniform, stayed until about 9.30 p.m. when all the cocoa lot were fully installed, then Andy walked her back to the nurses' home.

They always used to leave the door open. They were affectionate but never passionate. They toasted crumpets in front of the gas fir and cooked soup, baked beans and spaghetti on the gas ring. O'Sullivan was right, this was the best room in the hospital.

Mary was terribly worried about meeting his father and Auntie

Rob. "Do you think they'll like me?" said Mary.

"No," said Andy smiling, "they'll love you."

"Guess what I did today," said Mary.

"I give up," said Andy.

"I had some flowers sent to the Matron, she will never know who they're from. If she hadn't told me off, we might never be together, and although she's all-powerful now, think of the lonely spinstery life she and her cronies have, and what have they to look forward to? Just look at the happiness I have to look forward to with you.

"Oh, darling, I feel so lucky, it all seems too good to be true, pinch me and tell me I'm not dreaming."

"No," said Andy, "I'll kiss you instead. Sometimes you look like a smiling pixie, I could eat you. I know someone who is much luckier than you."

"Impossible," said Mary, "who is this luckiest of people?"

"Why me, you idiot," said Andy.

The day they set out to meet his father and Aunty Rob Andy didn't tease her, she looked terribly pale and tense. She was wearing a smart suit, felt hat, lace-up shoes and carried some flowers. "You look so elegant my love," said Andy.

"Are you sure," she replied, "my stomach is doing cartwheels. Are you sure your father and aunt won't mind you getting married to an orphan Annie."

Andy said, "Darling, they'll love you. They'll be worrying now about what you will think of them."

Andy so wished his mother was alive, Mary could have been just the person to melt her.

His father met them at the station, there was no awkwardness, Mary just ran up to him and embraced him. You would have thought it was a daughter coming home from school. They talked as if they were continuing an interrupted conversation. Andy stood back watching.

"What do I call you?" said Mary, "Mr Howard sounds so formal."

"You just call me dad," said his father.

Mary went up and gave his father another hug, but this time it was to hide the tears that were forming.

They got into his father's car. "Do you mind if we just pop up and see your mother's grave?" said his father. "Auntie Rob said lunch won't be until one sharp, she doesn't want to be interrupted."

They drove to the churchyard, then walked up towards his mother's grave, Mary taking his father's arm, and placing the flowers that she'd really meant for Auntie Rob, on his mother's grave. She said to his father, "Andy said his mother was a fine actress."

"She was a fine woman," said his father, "sadly we spent too much time shouting."

As they motored up the drive, there was Auntie Rob hopping from one foot to another in her excitement. She just about devoured Mary, embracing her, then standing back she said, "Andy, you've got a winner."

Auntie Rob's Sunday lunch was better than usual, even her Yorkshire pudding was improving. Any worry or inhibition Mary might have had was soon dispelled as they were all chattering six to the dozen. Mary and Auntie Rob washed up while Andy went through to the lounge with his father.

"She's quite lovely in every way," said his father, "you're a lucky boy."

They all gathered in the lounge and Mary and Andy were bombarded with questions. When were they going to get married, when and where were they going for their honeymoon.?

"Well," said Andy, "we've decided it's either going to be St Paul's Cathedral or Ealing Town Hall for the wedding and, of course, the honeymoon will be a round the world cruise."

"Don't forget you can have Instow if you like for your honeymoon," said Auntie Rob.

"Oh, I would love that," said Mary, "I've heard so much about it. Could we Andy?"

"Of course we could," said Andy. "Thank you Auntie Rob." Auntie Rob went quite pink with pleasure.

Andy showed Mary round the house and garden, then to his bedroom where there was a pile of all sorts of toys in a heap on the floor. "Do you think," he said, "it would be appropriate if we took them with us when we go to see the Master and Mother of your Home in two weeks' time?"

"I didn't know we were going there," said Mary.

"It's me being masterful," said Andy.

"No," said Mary, biting her lip, "you're just perfect." She paused, "no, just you and I will go the first time, bless you, we'll take the toys another time."

The Sunday just whizzed past. Auntie Rob insisted that Mary went into her house to look at some treasures with her. Andy suddenly realized that he had never ever been in Auntie Rob's house.

Eventually the time came to go. "I shall always remember this happy day," said Mary to Andy's father when he dropped them off at the station. On the train they snuggled up together holding hands, and Andy always found that holding hands with Mary had a quality all its own. Her smooth, cool hands, slipped into his, was what the Chinese called, 'a wave of a thousand comforts'.

When they got back to the hospital, Mary came up for cocoa. There was a note on his table, Matron would like to see him in her office at 1 p.m. the next day.

"She's not going to stop me coming up here," said Mary, "I wonder if I've got a note too?"

When he went back with her, Andy waited outside the nurses' home for Mary to pop up and see if she had a note too. She came down waving a piece of paper. "Yes, I'm for the chop too, but just let her dare try to stop me seeing you." She kissed him. "You and your family are such loves," she said.

"No," said Andy, "they're not my family, they are our family. See you tomorrow."

At 1 p.m. on the dot they arrived outside Matron's office, knocked, and a stern voice said, "Come in. Sit you both down." In an unfamiliar tone Matron said, "Well, you both know there is a rule that nurses do not visit doctors' rooms." Mary was just about to reply when Matron raised her hand to silence her. "In the case of you two, you do it with my blessing. I was engaged to a Houseman once, but he was killed at Dunkirk so I've devoted myself to being an old crab. Grab every precious moment and happiness you can and don't forget, I'm here if you want me. Your Mother at the children's home often talks on the phone young Mary. Now be off with you."

The two were quite knocked off their guard, not knowing what to say, they just couldn't say, "thank you Matron". Words did come to Andy. "I'm so sorry about your fiancé, Matron, we do appreciate how lucky we are."

As they reached the door Matron said, "By the way Mary, florists can't keep secrets any more, I was very touched by your flowers."

As they walked away from the office they were both quiet. Then Andy said, "Really I expect she's nicer than either of us."

"No," said Mary, "there's no one nicer than you."

"Oh yes there is," said Andy, "you are."

"Well," said Mary seriously, "you never know what is happening in other people's lives, I feel quite humble. In my own life, I can't remember anything before the time you took me to the ball."

"You're a pixie not a Cinderella," said Andy, "you can't be both."

"I'll just settle for being your wife-to-be," said Mary, and gave Andy a peck and went off towards the children's ward.

A few nights later they were sitting having cocoa when Andy said, "God, the medical finals start on Monday."

"Have you entered," said Mary.

"Yes, and paid," said Andy, "but I haven't looked at a book or anything for a year, it's not worth going."

"Love," said Mary, "in the annals of medical history no knight in shining armour has been failed any medical exam anywhere, you have nothing to lose."

"As your ladyship commands," said Andy, "but we are still going to your home at the weekend."

The Master and Mother, a plump, late middle-aged couple had been father and mother to literally hundreds of children, they almost shone with goodness. Andy was a bit isolated from the conversation, but there was little doubt that Mary had always been special to them, and they agreed to come to the wedding be it Ealing Register Office or St Paul's Cathedral.

At his fourth attempt Andy sailed through his degree medicine. By now he was a pretty experienced doctor, and, of course, as Mary said, "Knights in shining armour never fail exams." So he was now Dr Andrew Howard, MB, BS, LMSSA. He didn't feel any different.

His first job on hearing of his success was to inject somebody's piles. Mary said, "I thought a highly qualified man like you could have chosen something better than that to start with."

"No," said Andy, "it's always best to start at the bottom." Mary threw a cushion at him.

It was Easter and they decided to take a picnic to Box Hill. "Perhaps in the clear air," she said, "we can make some plans for the future."

As usual Andy had been working hell for leather, and sometimes they even had to miss the odd hour they usually had together in the evenings.

It was a brisk spring day and they brought a car rug which they sat on, and they both kept their coats on. "Can we look at the overall plan," said Mary. "I'd marry you tomorrow if I could, but I must pass my SRN, I promised Mother and the Master that I would, and they were so good to me, but at the same time I just don't want to let you out of my sight. I have two months and one year before I take my finals, there's no way I can expect you to stay at the hospital here, but I don't know if I can bear to be without you."

"I know just how you feel, love," said Andy, "and I feel the same way. I've only two months of this terrible job to finish, but I've got to do some obstetrics, preferably a job where I can get my diploma in obstetrics. Unlike you, that's another year and two months. Cocoa and crumpets for a year and two months is just not enough to me. There is a possibility that something might happen, but I daren't tell you about it my love. I'm going off to the West of England for a night next week, just to look at a job, don't ask me too much about it. It may not come off. It may not be what we want, but on the other hand, it might be."

"Oh, love," said Mary, "you're going so far away."

"Shush," said Andy, putting his finger to her lips, "just wait and see."

A week later Andy got on the train to go to Barnstaple in North Devon. He had heard from another Houseman, who had been down to see it, that it offered obstetrics and a two bedroom furnished flat where 'you could flick a fly rod into the river Taw from the bedroom window'. The hospital had difficulty filling the job because, although it was partly obstetrics, there was not enough to take a diploma, but enough to get on the general practice obstetrics list to practice obstetrics, and this was always essential for a junior partner.

It was a lovely journey down through the countryside. He had to change at Exeter for Barnstaple, and, looking at the empty fields on either side, he wondered, as the train thundered on, whether anybody lived in England at all. The North Devon Infirmary was an old hospital. Its Consultant staff were also general practitioners, although most of them had higher qualifications. The job offered was in obstetrics, general surgery, ENTs, with Casualty duties. There were only three staff at the hospital, one Senior House Officer and two pre-Registration, one a House Physician and one a House Surgeon. He was interviewed by a very nice surgeon, a Mr Shaw, and a young 'very with it' physician, Rex King.

"A fine job for getting into general practice, but not much chance of getting into a practice down here," said Rex King. "Do you know the area?"

"Oh, I've had a holiday at Instow," said Andy.

"Well, we've seen your references, this is a difficult job to fill, go and have a look at the accommodation and if you want it, the job is yours."

"Is it possible for me to speak to the Matron while I'm here, my fiancé hasn't finished her training yet," said Andy.

"By all means," said Rex King, "I'll take you over, she lives in the flat below where you'll be living if you do come."

Andy was taken over and introduced to a tiny Welsh woman who was less like a Matron than he'd ever seen. He explained Mary's problem. Would there be any chance of her completing the last year of her SRN's training in Barnstaple if they were married?"

"I don't see any problem," said the Matron, "I'll go and ring St Daniel's." She was back in about half an hour. "All's fixed," she said, "but we'll leave it to you to break the news to your fiancé. We do hope you will come, I'm sure you'll love it down here."

The train couldn't hurry back quick enough for Andy. He'd had to spend a restless night in a local hotel and he caught the earliest train he could in the morning. He kept out of Mary's way during the day until late in the afternoon he popped into the children's ward and said, "Cocoa?"

"About 6 o'clock," said Mary. "I've got some good news."

"So have I," said Andy.

"Oh lovely," said Mary.

Andy had the pan already on the gas ring by the time Mary came to his room. This pan was multi-purpose, as they used it to cook cocoa, soup, spaghetti, and boiled eggs. One day, one of the Housemen went to the Ideal Home Exhibition and at evening cocoa time said, "Andy, I've been to the Ideal Home Exhibition, toured every stall, and have brought you back the most valuable possession I can think of."

"That's very nice of you," said Andy, surprised — it was a packet of scourers!

When Mary came in she was holding a large official envelope. "Oh darling," she said, "you seem to have been away years."

"I know," said Andy, "but I'm back. Now then," he said, "your good news first."

"Well," Mary said, "it's unbelievable," and she opened the envelope and in it were the deeds of Auntie Rob's Instow cottage. She was giving her the Instow cottage as a wedding present.

"That's wonderful," said Andy, "we're property owners now," and he said, "if ever I should go off and you should divorce me you'd always own half of it."

Mary went white, "Please Andy don't talk like that." She said, "I know I'm not a physical person and very demonstrative, but I love you so deeply it hurts. I shall always love you whatever you do. I know how disappointed you were not getting into the Army, but I am ashamed to say I was overjoyed because I thought that I'd see more of you.

"I remember one day after the ball when I saw you playing with little Amy on the ward — this was before I knew you — I just had to stop myself coming up and saying, 'please let me bear your children,' oh, I do want to Andy. I said I'd had a wonderful childhood, and I did, but I also had bad experiences. Three of us went for adoption once, my two best friends and I, and we were inspected like goods for sale. My two best friends were taken and I wasn't, and in come way I've felt rejected ever since. That's why I say that I can't bear to be away from you, having found you I don't ever want to let you go." She was sobbing now.

"Oh my love," said Andy, "I'm so sorry, come over on the armchair and sit on my knee."

She cuddled up with her forehead pressed under his chin like a little girl. "Oh I'm sorry," said Mary, "I know that there was no way you'd want to upset me, but I so love going to your family. To think, I might be part of it, and we have all these frustrations ahead of us. There's a year and two months. I don't think I can live without you for a year and two months. I might have to let the Master and Mother down."

"You won't have to," said Andy.

"I will if I can't be with you all the time."

"Well, perhaps you can be with me all the time."

Mary sat up. "Yes, you haven't told me your good news."

"Well," said Andy, "with your approval, in three months' time I accept a Senior House Officer job at the North Devon Infirmary, Barnstaple, where there is a self-contained flat overlooking the river. The Matrons have got together and the Matron at Barnstaple and the Matron here are quite happy for you to do your final year at Barnstaple. It's just like a dream, and with Auntie Rob giving us the cottage at Instow, we will always have a base. Unless you have any objections Mary Smith, I intend to marry you in eight weeks' time and have a month's honeymoon with you at Instow before we move to the flat in Barnstaple as man and wife where I will do obstetrics and you will finish your nursing."

Mary was silent for much longer than she ought to have been. "Are things all right with you?" said Andy. "Aren't you happy about it?"

"Yes, my love, it's more than I could possibly ever have wished for, even in my wildest dreams. I was just very sincerely saying a prayer for all those people who haven't been as fortunate as we are."

"I have one disappointment for you." said Andy.

"I don't think you have any disappointments for me," said Mary.

"Oh yes," said Andy, mockingly, "there is a very serious one. I cannot get St Paul's Cathedral in eight weeks' time, so it looks like the Ealing Register Office in Ealing Town Hall, and if you want to, we have got to get busy and start making arrangements to turn you into Mrs Howard. I am going to count to ten and during those ten seconds you have to decide whether you are going to be my partner for life."

Mary turned her head this way and that way, grinning as if she was having to make a great decision. "All right then," she said, and with a different voice, "I promise my love, I will always take the greatest care of you. I've watched people here take advantage of you, you're just too kind and too nice and you work so very hard, but aren't we so lucky?"

"Yes," said Andy. "Like you, I can hardly believe it, but it is true and there will be times when we won't be as lucky as we are now, and we must remember this time when everything seems to be working for us. Let's say the Gods made the sun to shine on us."

"What all of them," said Mary.

"Yes," said Andy, "every single one of them."

CHAPTER 10

WEDDING BELLS

During the last two months at St Daniel's Andy paid less attention to his medical work than he had ever done, or ever did for the rest of his medical life. The wedding and Mary took up every spare moment of his time. They had chosen Ealing Register Office to get married in as Andy had once attended the wedding of one of his Rugby mates there. Although Ealing Town Hall looked a bit grimy from the outside, inside the reception and wedding room were elegant and the Registrar, a delightful kindly lady, made sure the ceremony was carried out with dignity.

At least half of the 1st XV of St Jane's Hospital Rugby XV had got married in Register Offices and Andy had attended them all. With one exception, the brides were all with child before the wedding.

The sites and ceremonies of most of the weddings were appalling. Often there had been a queue, and it was more like having a passport stamped than getting married.

Andy had never forgotten the occasion at Ealing and was determined that this was where he was going to marry Mary.

They rang the Town Hall to fix the date, and a nice receptionist pointed out that they first had to come and make an appointment bringing their Birth Certificates, and had they residential qualifications?

"We have both lived in England all our lives," said Andy.

"No," said the receptionist patiently, "you have to have lived in the borough of Ealing at least 17 days."

"Oh, that's no problem," said Andy, knowing that it was a tremendous problem. "When I've got my duties sorted out we will ring again."

"Oh, love," he said to Mary explaining the full gist of his call. "We have to be resident in Ealing for 17 days before we are allowed to fix a date."

"Never mind darling," said Mary, "let's have a look at what they offer locally, it might be OK. What I hate, is having to show my Birth Certificate, against father and mother it says unknown."

"Darling," said Andy, "you are about to become the head of a dynasty and that will never happen to your children, your grandchildren or your great grandchildren."

"Idiot," said Mary, "now my life's gone by in a flash."

They found their nearest Register Office. It was only 200 yards from the hospital and it was just dreadful. "I expect it doubles as an abattoir when they're not using it for weddings," said Andy. They trudged back to the hospital in gloomy silence. O'Sullivan was standing on the steps.

"Where are those smiling faces of the bride and bridegroom of the year?" said O'Sullivan.

"Don't," said Andy, "we've struck problems. We can't be married in Ealing until we've been resident 17 days, and there is no way either of us can manage that within the next eight weeks, and down the road is more like a funeral parlour."

"Ealing's no problem, man," said O'Sullivan, "all you babes in the wood have to do is to leave a case at my Auntie Bessie's in Ealing. Tonight if you want, and in 17 days you can choose your day."

"Is that all right?" asked Andy.

"Would you ever doubt O'Sullivan," said O'Sullivan.

"You're just marvellous," said Mary, and kissed him.

"That makes you a Jamaican citizen," said O'Sullivan.

Andy and Mary set off for Aunt Bessie's with a suitcase full of old shirts and socks. They were slightly apprehensive having seen O'Sullivan's residence with thirty to a room as to what they were walking into, but Aunt Bessie's house was a large terraced house in Darwin Road, South Ealing where only she and her pastor gospel-preaching husband lived. They had the warmest of welcomes with repeated 'Bless yous', an offer from Uncle Keithley, Aunt Bessie's husband, to marry them in their front room which doubled as a church meeting place if they had problems with Ealing Town Hall.

"The trouble is," said Andy, when they were cuddled up in his room drinking cocoa, "most people think doctors are worldly wise and they're not, they know little of what is going on in the world outside the hospital."

"Rubbish," said Mary, kissing the side of his face. She had an arm round his neck and was holding a mug of cocoa precariously in her hand. "You are the wisest man in the world."

"Only when it comes to choosing brides," said Andy, returning her kiss and spilling her cocoa at the same time.

They were most courteously received at Ealing Register Office. They had waited a month before going and Aunt Bessie, who the office knew, came with them. They were able to fix the exact date they wanted — three days after Andy's resident job finished and five days after Mary completed her second year exams.

Presents rolled in. The whole hospital had taken them to heart. They even had a decanter and glasses from Mr Gotter. They began by stacking things in Andy's room then Andy's father ran a shuttle service taking them to a room Auntie Rob had cleared for them in her house.

Andy's father bought him a suit and gave him a hundred pounds.

Andy was worried about Mary and money. He had no idea if she had enough money for all the things she would need.

"Darling I'm fine," she said, "I have been saving for this since I was ten, and in addition to the Instow Cottage, Auntie Rob keeps on sending me more than little amounts which I am banking. In fact, I am becoming a wealthy woman and I'm just wondering if you are only marrying me for my money."

Time flew. There was a hen night and a bachelor night, both a few days before the wedding, not the night before. Andy looked round at the dozen companions who were sharing his so-called last night of freedom. Only a couple were from his Rugby days. It was just two years since he had qualified, yet he had almost lost touch with his student contemporaries. There was one cousin he hardly knew, the rest were all from St Daniel's, mainly the cocoa drinkers or the 'United Nations' as they called themselves, with representatives from Australia, New Zealand, India, Pakistan, Poland, Ireland, Jamaica and the Lebanon.

After a very heavy night they all finished up at O'Sullivan's drinking white rum. In the past Andy had thought he'd had a few hangovers after Rugby games, but after this night, he really learnt what a hangover was. Thank God the wedding wasn't the next day.

They had great trouble in sorting out who to ask. The whole hospital wanted to come. In the end they settled for six nurses, Matron was asked but declined in the nicest possible way, and gave them a tea set which they felt had come from what had been her own bottom drawer.

The Master and Mother were bringing a dozen girls from the children's home to the ceremony, then staying on themselves for the reception that Andy's father had arranged in a restaurant across the road from the Town Hall.

Andy had an Aunt whom he hardly knew whose son had come to his bachelor night. David Hudson was to be his best man and the Master of the children's home was giving Mary away. There were Mr and Mrs O'Sullivan, of course, and Aunt Bessie and Mr Keithley, most of the 'United Nations', three married Rugby players, their spouses and babies, and sundry friends and hangers-on.

The reception, which was going to be limited to thirty for their quiet wedding, grew to sixty. Andy's father was quite happy about it but they couldn't ask any more as the restaurant only held sixty.

Andy never knew how much money his father had. Their house was nice, but modestly furnished, his cars were usually elderly, and since his mother died seven years ago, his father had led the quietest of lives. Only over the last two years had his father and Auntie Rob been on one or two coach holidays together.

The most excited person about the marriage was, of course, Auntie Rob. She had given Mary a room of her own to use in the pre-wedding preparations and to stay in for a couple of nights before the wedding and, of course, there was a room that she'd let them have for presents.

The first time Andy had ever been in Auntie Rob's house was when he went in to look at the accumulating presents. It was like a gingerbread house, all chintz and ornaments. He hardly dared turn round in case he knocked something over. An unkind person would have called it 'fussy' but it wasn't. It was just Auntie Rob's house.

On the last day of May they went round the hospital saying

goodbye to everybody. There were tears, hugs and more presents. To his surprise, Andy found O'Sullivan crying. "Oh God man, we're gonna miss you, we'll have no one to defend us in Casualty now."

Andy's father had come to take them home. They had dinner with him. Andy and Mary sat up late talking and then she slipped off to Auntie Rob's for the night.

The next day they hardly saw each other and Mary was busy doing last minute shopping with Auntie Rob and Andy was fixing train tickets. He had reserved seats for the train to Instow via Paddington, Exeter and Barnstaple. "Now, that's the last you see of her, young Andy, until tomorrow."

"Oh, come of it," said Andy, "surely."

"No," said Auntie Rob, "it's unlucky to see the bride the night before her wedding."

"Night, night my love," said Andy as they went to the door about 6 o'clock, "think, this time tomorrow you'll be Mrs Howard."

"I can't wait," said Mary.

Andy slept fretfully that night, and most of his thoughts were not about Mary, but about his mother and how she would have loved to have been there. He hadn't realized that with her having been dead for seven years, he could still miss her so much. He awoke on his wedding morning not rested, but this was a day when the sun did shine for the bride, it was lovely, the 3rd June, his mother's birthday.

He bathed, shaved carefully, put on his new suit and some new shoes he'd bought himself. "Very smart," said his father.

His father had got an old morning suit out which Andy didn't think would be appropriate for the type of ceremony they were going to, but said nothing. He was dying to see Mary and wondered what she looked like. As it was a Register Office they would be going together. They had hired a wedding car and his father and Auntie Rob were going to go on ahead of them to find a parking place.

He waited impatiently until about half past ten then excited, twittering, Auntie Rob came knocking on the door. "Right," she said, "you can come and see your beautiful bride now." Various people such as hairdressers and florists had been coming and going to Auntie Rob's. Andy just had a white carnation in his buttonhole.

"Come on," said Auntie Rob as Andy hesitated.

She led him into her lounge and there was Mary.

Andy almost choked, she looked so utterly beautiful. Her fair hair had been threaded with flowers, she was wearing a white linen calf-length dress, her arms were bare and she had a bouquet of mixed carnations.

"Darling," he said, "you look so beautiful."

"Don't you dare make me cry," she said, "otherwise my mascara will run down my cheeks and I'll have to go and start getting dressed again."

As they drove towards the Register Office they thought there must be some special event on, as there were crowds of people outside the hall. As they drew nearer they could hear a steel band playing. "It's bloody O'Sullivan," said Andy, and there were crowds in the street waving and they felt like royalty. They had almost to fight their way through into the reception area, which again was crammed with people, then into the room where the ceremony was to take place. Twelve excited little girls from the children's home were in the front row. The room was tastefully furnished and the Registrar was elegantly dressed. As they went through the ceremony Andy kept on taking little glances at Mary, he just couldn't believe how beautiful she looked.

They signed the register and it was witnessed, then they sat in the Registrar's chair and had their photographs taken. Uncle Keithley got up and felt he ought to bless the wedding in the name of the Lord and the Registrar very kindly made no objection. The official photographer came, more photographs on the steps of the Town Hall and confetti covering the pavement under the sign which said 'No Confetti'. Fortunately the reception was in a restaurant just across the road. It all seemed unreal to Andy, but Mary gripped his hand so tightly it gave him the comfort he needed, as well as pins and needles.

They had a simple meal at the restaurant, melon, ham salad and trifle. They all had a sherry when they went in and there was some sparkling wine for the toasts and the cake.

Eventually the hire car came to take them back to Auntie Rob's to change. They left the restaurant in a further shower of confetti. When they got back Mary disappeared to change and then in about fifteen minutes came out in a dazzling scarlet suit. She looked tremendous but to Andy's disappointment had taken the flowers from her hair. "Oh love," he said, "you look absolutely gorgeous, but couldn't you have kept those flowers in your hair, they looked quite regal?"

"No," said Mary, "everybody would have thought you had married a florist."

The chauffeur and the hire car had waited to take them to Paddington. His father and Auntie Rob arrived just in time to say a last goodbye before they left. The chauffeur carried their cases from the hire car to the train. Andy stopped outside the first class carriage.

"What are we doing here?" said Mary.

"Nothing but the best for you today, my love," said Andy. So they sat in the splendour of a first class carriage. They went to the Pullman Car for dinner and gazed out over the endless countryside as they sped towards Exeter.

Mary said, "I think England is uninhabited." Apart from a few cows and sheep they hardly saw a single person between Paddington and Exeter.

They drew into St David's Station and waited on the platform for the connection to Barnstaple and Instow, which was a bit of an anticlimax. It was getting dark by now, and as they approached Instow all they could see were the street lamps.

As they approached Instow Mary became very tense. There were no taxis at the station so they had to carry their cases for a couple of hundred yards to what was now their home. It was just a dark shape and Mary was strangely silent as Andy unlocked the door. They carried the cases in, Andy leading, and as he switched on the light he heard Mary's sharp intake of breath. Andy turned, she was looking white and tense.

"Darling," she said, "would you be very understanding and leave me on my own for a few minutes?"

Andy was taken aback, but Mary was so tense and serious he said, "Of course my love," and went off into the lounge.

Mary stood in the hall for about five minutes, then he heard her wandering through all the rooms of the house accompanied by the small sounds that people make when they pick up objects to examine them and then replace them. She was gone at least a quarter of an hour and Andy had become seriously worried about her when she came into the lounge, tears streaming down her face, and clung to Andy sobbing.

"Oh my love," said Andy, "have I upset you?"

"No darling," said Mary slowly composing herself, "I just feel I'm in a fairy-tale. I have been looking around at every nook and cranny of our own house. For the first time in my life I have a home of my very own, and, Oh, my dearest, dearest love, I have you. I am truly the luckiest girl in the world."

"Well," said Andy relieved, "you happen to be holding on to the luckiest man in the world."

They stood for a while holding each other until Mary said, "As a good housewife I must get my house in order."

They began to unpack and put things away. In the kitchen were boxes of goods previously ordered in by Auntie Rob, and enough to feed an army for six months. Mary made sure that everything was unpacked and put in its proper place. There were continual squeals of pleasure as she discovered things she had missed on her first tour of inspection. At last they were finished. They had a cup of cocoa, cuddled up together in the lounge in front of the gas fire and then to bed, exhausted.

On their first morning Andy was woken by Mary bringing in a tray of tea. In the background there was a noise of surf breaking on the beach and seagulls squabbling.

"No tea in bed this morning, I have to show you the real treasures of the house," said Andy. He slipped on his dressing gown and went outside to move wooden protective shutters from the lounge windows. He came back in, opened the doors and pulled two deck-chairs and a small table out on to the patio. Mary put the tea tray on the table and then took in the panoramic view. The Appledore lifeboat was swinging on its moorings, the trawler, *The Lundy Gannet*, was on its way to Lundy, trying to beat the tide, and the John Bros. ferry was making its way slowly from Instow to Appledore.

"Oh love," she said, "is all this true? Do you know that this is only one of the few times I have actually seen the sea, it is unbelievable, I feel I'm in a dream. I'm collecting each precious moment just in case something awful comes along to stop it. The very best thing about it all is my most beloved husband. Darling, will you always love me?"

"Well, pixie," said Andy, "I can only guarantee it until you're eighty five, then you'll have to re-negotiate."

She managed to kiss him and pour a cup of tea at the same time. "Why do you call me pixie?" said Mary.

"Just because you are a pixie," said Andy, "you're far too nice to be a human. Perhaps one day we'll find a unicorn together and you can ride it along Instow sands."

"You're an idiot," said Mary. "What's the programme today?"

"Well," said Andy, "we have to rouse in three hours and make our way to the Marine Hotel for lunch, then we have to come back here and relax after our efforts and watch the world go by, but first I think we ought to have another snuggle in bed."

"It sounds perfect," said Mary, ruffling his hair.

This became the pattern they established over the next few days, patiently and tenderly getting to know each other. On about the fifth morning Andy woke with a start to find the bed beside him empty and strange noises coming from the kitchen. Not waiting to put on his dressing gown he rushed through, alarmed, bursting in the kitchen to find Mary dressed, hair tied up in a scarf, taking crockery out of a cupboard to add to the ever growing pile on the kitchen table.

"Are you all right love?" he queried.

"Of course," said Mary, "as soon as I've had my good morning kiss."

"Darling," she said, standing back, "please indulge me, I am fulfilling a lifetime's ambition, I'm being a housewife," and she repeated, "it is a lifetime's ambition."

"So," said Andy, "you want to spend your honeymoon doing housework."

"It sounds silly," said Mary, "but I expect in a way I do, so please don't be cross."

"I'll make one condition," said Andy.

"Anything," said Mary.

"Promise," said Andy.

"Anything, I promise," said Mary.

"Well," said Andy, "I would like to be your first lieutenant and help you."

"Oh Andy," said Mary, "you're such a love, these last few days have been heaven, but I've been itching to get my fingers on this, our own house, I want to scrub it from top to bottom and wash all the sheets and curtains. Fancy, I could have a whole line of washing flapping in the breeze, plus, I want to eat you for breakfast, lunch and tea. I nearly asked you last night if I could start to spring clean, but it would have sounded so silly."

"My love," said Andy, "I am with you all the way. It is now 7.30 a.m., let's go back to bed for an early breakfast."

People spend their honeymoons in different ways, few devote it to spring cleaning. For two weeks they turned out the house from top to bottom, the washing line was always full. They went by bus to Bideford and Barnstaple shopping. Andy couldn't keep his eyes off Mary, he had never seen anyone so sublimely happy.

The bulk of their shopping was done from the Post Office stores in Instow where they were soon regulars. One day a tall smiling, handsome-looking lady introduced herself in the shop as Margaret King, wife of Rex King, one of the Consultants who had interviewed Andy when he went up for the job at the North Devon Infirmary. She said that she hoped they would come and have dinner with her once they were installed in the North Devon Infirmary.

"I don't have to ask if you are enjoying your honeymoon," she said, "you could not look happier."

"It's just been wonderful," said Mary, "we've been ..." and if Andy hadn't pressed his foot hard on hers, she would have plunged into the spring cleaning, laundry, et cetera. She managed to tail off her sentence rather tamely saying, "We've just been pottering about having a lazy time."

"Well, make the most of it," said Margaret King, "the rest of married life is just hard work. See you soon," and strode out of the shop.

"Thank you darling," said Mary as they walked home, "she would have thought I was a loony if I had really told her what we've been doing. Has it been all right darling? When I look at things from a distance I have been so selfish, what about you, you've been so patient, has it been what you've wanted?"

"There's only one thing I want," said Andy, "and that is you're just never out of my sight, I've loved every minute of it. It's what you and I want. What other people want or think doesn't matter. I usually make a mess of things, I'm a sort of walking disaster, the most successful thing I have ever done in my life is to persuade you to marry me," and he kissed her on the nose, "I will cherish you."

"Vice versa," said Mary, "I feel so lucky it's like achieving one's wildest dream and finding it's even better than you thought it possible."

Andy stood back looking at her. "There's something we must do straightaway," he said.

"What?" queried Mary.

"Dash back, put on our bathing costumes and jump into the sea, otherwise," he said, "we're going to spontaneously combust."

They ran back to the house hand in hand laughing like a couple of children.

They were walking along the beach, their arms around each other after dusk settled over the estuary and lights in Appledore across the water began to twinkle.

"Is that the moon shining over there?" said Mary.

"No," said Andy, "it's your ultra clean house shining."

"Ouch," he said as Mary pushed him into a puddle.

"I was wanting to say something serious, or rather ask something serious," said Mary.

"I know," said Andy.

"You can't know," said Mary.

"But I do know," said Andy.

"All right, clever clogs," said Mary, "tell me what I was going to say."

"You were going to suggest that we ask Auntie Rob and my father down for our last week."

"That's incredible," said Mary, "you read my mind."

"It's quite easy," said Andy, "all I have to do is to work out what is the nicest possible thought you could have, then name it."

"God, I love you," said Mary.

"Vice versa," said Andy, "and what is more, I completely agree with you.

"It really would be lovely, our first guests. Oh darling," said Mary, jumping with excitement, "when can we ask them?"

Andy replied, "I spy a phone box two hundred yards down the

road."

The excitement back at home was almost overwhelming. They rang Auntie Rob whose squeaks could be heard down the Instow Prom. She had rushed next door to fetch Andy's father. They had just enough time to decide that they'd be coming down in two days, before Andy ran out of coins.

The next two days were a frenzy of cleaning and shopping. At last the day came with Andy and Mary popping out and looking to see if they were coming. Then suddenly, they arrived and it was all embraces, kissing, and everybody talking. Mary took Auntie Rob off on a tour of inspection, while Andy made a pot of tea.

It was the beginning of another wonderful week and with a car they were able to explore all the local beauty spots, Clovelly, Ilfracombe, the beaches of Croyde, Woolacombe, Westward Ho!, Barnstaple, Bideford, Lynton and Lynmouth, with cream teas in most of them. Mary was turning out to be the daughter that Auntie Rob had never had, and the one his father had always wanted. Mary's happiness was complete now she had real parents who loved her.

Andy used to watch her as she and Auntie Rob clucked round the house doing housewifely things. His father was content to stretch out in a deck chair and watch the goings on on the river.

On the last day of their honeymoon he moved them to their furnished flat in the North Devon Infirmary. It was a spacious three bedroom flat. They knew that they would be able to go to Instow for at least one night a week when Andy had his half day, and every third weekend from Friday night to Monday morning. During their year at the North Devon Infirmary they were to have a month's holiday, so the move was less painful than it could have been.

Auntie Rob and his father were staying on at Instow for a further week. With Auntie Rob making quite sure that it was Mary who had invited her to stay, she wasn't assuming that she had any right to the property.

Alone in the flat, Andy took stock then said, "Well, my love it's work tomorrow."

"But you love your work darling," said Mary.

"Yes, perhaps," said Andy, as he took her in his arms, "but I love you a great deal more."

CHAPTER 11

ONE OF EACH

The North Devon Infirmary was a lovely old building, much older than St Daniel's and, like St Daniel's, needed a great deal of money spent on it. Unlike St Daniel's though, everything was neat and clean. The vast majority of the nursing staff were local, and all the consulting staff were general practitioners, even though they all sported specialist qualifications, FRCS, MRCP and one FRCP. There was a happy atmosphere of kindness and caring. Both Andy and Mary settled in immediately.

The resident hospital staff consisted of Andy, Senior House Officer, or Junior Registrar if you wanted to flatter him, and both a preRegistration House Physician and House Surgeon - in this case, both girls doing their first hospital jobs. In addition to all his many duties, Andy had to see the girls through procedures like lumber punctures, putting up drips and giving simple anaesthetics in Casualty, in much the same way that David Hudson had instructed him in his first job at St Daniel's.

The new aspect of Andy's work was obstetrics and gynaecology. He had done his routine twenty deliveries as a student at St Jane's but that seemed a hundred years ago.

The North Devon Infirmary only took in abnormal deliveries often very abnormal.

There were only twelve maternity beds in the hospital to serve an area stretching from Bude in North Cornwall to Lynton and Lynmouth. There was no way you could just decide to come into hospital and have your baby just because you wanted to. Unless there was some complication, it was a home birth or in one of the maternity nursing homes scattered through the district, many of which had virtually no equipment, but they did have electric light and running water, which was not always available at home. In his early general practice days, Andy always swore that he'd delivered by the light of a burning faggot.

At the Infirmary Andy learnt how to put on forceps, and was even allowed to do a Caesarean operation before his year was up.

Mary had been put as a Senior Nurse on Fortescue Ward under the care of the short, almost square, bespectacled Sister Sweet who was sweet by name and sweet by nature. Mary was impressed by the friendliness of everyone, both nurses and patients. It took her a little while to realize that most of the staff knew many of the patients outside the hospital and were answerable to them and their families in and out of hospital. There was a lot to be said for this formula, it led to the high standard of care both nursing and medical.

Andy and Mary did not fraternize in the hospital itself, and the fact that she was the wife of a doctor did not inhibit her colleagues. She soon made friends, and before long the flat was full of nurses and their boyfriends enjoying parties and trips to the beach. Andy and Mary tended not to ask people out to Instow, keeping this precious portion of time to themselves. They were both very busy and very happy.

The midwifery, which took up a lot of Andy's time, was one area of medicine where you could almost guarantee a happy ending. The two pre-Registration House girls, Pamela and Alice, were both hard workers but were, of course, inexperienced and needed a lot of mothering, Alice more than Pam.

Both Dr and Mrs King were very kind to Andy and Mary, often having them to meals. Margaret King had been a nurse and living close to Instow they were the privileged two who did get invited to Andy and Mary's home. Andy thought that Rex was the best instinctive diagnostician he had ever met and throughout his medical career he never met his equal.

The weeks flew by. They loved the precious weekends when they were able to get to the house at Instow. Mary was always doing something to improve it, painting, putting up curtains, and prowling round secondhand and antique shops and, after storms, beach combing, so the house gradually began to fill up with glass fishing floats, corks from nets and pieces of wood in such strange shapes that they could have been sculpted.

It was soon summer to enjoy a whole month off, the hospital getting a locum to cover Andy's absence. Auntie Rob and his father came down for the first week, and they were no intrusion. It was such a pleasure to have them and to see their pleasure in coming. Auntie Rob had baked enough food to last them months, and in addition, she'd brought a host of other presents.

Andy remembered how, before his mother's death, they almost scorned this lonely widow who was their neighbour, nothing malicious was intended, it was just the way people who have lost their partners tend to be treated. Perhaps as a single person they offer a sort of threat, a loose missile. Even people like Auntie Rob, who was no threat to anyone. Safely married couples clung together. When they lost a partner, friends or neighbours initially did everything they could to help and support them, then tended to veer away and treated them as if they were odd, often creating eccentrics. But now Auntie Rob had an escort in Andy's father, a most beloved daughter in Mary and a loved son in Andy. She'd never been happier and life had never been fuller.

It was a good summer and for the next three weeks after they'd gone Andy and Mary were almost continually in their swimming things. With the help of Auntie Rob and his father they had acquired a dinghy with an outboard motor and a lug sail. They went up the Torridge on the tide as far as Weare Gifford for picnics and cream teas and down river on a calm day over the Bar to fish for mackerel. They had a day on Lundy Island travelling there and back on the

Lundy Gannet, climbing up the steep cliff to the plateau with the pub, the church, a few cottages, wild goats, peacocks and some cattle.

A few days before their holiday was due to end, Mary said plaintively, "Couldn't we stay here for ever?"

"Sadly there's no chance, my love," said Andy, "there is not likely to be a vacancy in the practice around here for years, I've been looking. It's down to poring through the Medical Journals when we get back. I have to learn to drive and we have to acquire a car."

"Oh dear," said Mary, "that reminds me, I've got my finals in four months, I know I shall fail."

Andy took her face in his hands and said, "In the whole course of human history it has never been known for the wife of a knight in shining armour to fail her nursing finals, especially when she is a pixie."

"You're just a gorgeous idiot," said Mary, "why do you keep on calling me pixie?"

"Just because you are a pixie," said Andy.

"You really are an idiot," said Mary, "and you make me so happy, if I were to die tomorrow."

Andy stopped her almost curtly. "Don't ever say that my love," and quite suddenly the room that had been filled with warmth and laughter seemed cold.

"I'm sorry," said Mary, "I forget sometimes about your mother, will you forgive me if I make you some egg and chips?"

"Only on one condition," said Andy.

"Anything," said Mary.

"Well, you must let me stick my chips in the yolk."

Life was still good when they returned to the North Devon Infirmary after their month's holiday, but not quite so good as it had been before. Great changes in their lives were looming ahead. Andy had been taking driving lessons, but he was not a natural and failed his first test. Now there was a panic with extra lessons to get him through by the end of the year. This was essential if they were to go into general practice as they hoped. Some of his weekends off were taken up going for interviews for practice vacancies. He was singularly unsuccessful, except on one occasion when having obviously failed in his interview, and not much liking the partners who interviewed him, having reached the surgery door to leave, was called back to find the attitude of the partners completely changed, now almost subservient.

"Excuse me," said the senior partner, in the friendliest of tones, "are you by chance *the* Dr Andrew Howard who hooked for the St Jane's Rugby team?"

"Yes," said Andy, puzzled.

"Well," said the senior partner, almost incontinent with excitement, "the post here is yours if you want it."

Andy floundered, tried to look keen, thanked them profusely and said how grateful he was but that he would just have to consult his wife. He left beaming faces, knowing full well there was no way he would go there again. He got back to Barnstaple as quickly as he could. When he got back in the flat with Mary she couldn't believe it.

"Do you mean to say they changed their minds just because you were good at hooking a ball out of the scrummage of players?"

"Yes," said Andy, "it makes you sick. Here we are desperate to get into general practice and the only one that invites me is not because I am a good doctor, it's because I was a good hooker. I wasn't even a good Rugby player."

They had, together, to write a most careful letter saying how sorry they were that they were not accepting this particular post.

Mary had seen Andy play Rugby. On two or three Saturdays, he played for Barnstaple, who had a first class team. He played for Barnstaple against Bideford in the local derby, Mary watching with Rex King. It was a real local derby, friendly but really tough, and Andy came out very bruised and battered, limping with one hand lacerated.

"You must make him stop this game," said Rex, "however much he loves it. Nobody in general practice wants a partner who can't use his legs and hands," and that was the last game Andy played.

Andy was almost in despair of finding a practice that he liked before his term at the North Devon Infirmary finished. Each week he scrutinized the pages of the *British Medical Journal*, nothing really interested him, and he didn't get interviews from those he wrote to. Then one week, unexpectedly there appeared the plummiest of all practices, not too many details about it, but it was Kangerford on the River Thames in the Thames Valley. He thought there would be thousands applying for it, but nothing ventured nothing gained, so he wrote off his usual letter. To his great surprise he was summoned for an interview. He went up by train and took a branch line from Reading to a small station called Cholsey, and then on to a tiny terminal line to Kangerford itself. He was able to walk down from the station, and having a few minutes to spare, he walked round this lovely little market town. He thought how lucky he would be to land this, but the chances must be just about nil.

Two very pleasant elderly doctors greeted him at their surgery which was a building in the grounds of a small community hospital. They were quite honest, they were both feeling their age, they wanted some new blood to do their midwifery and perhaps a great deal of the night calls. They offered him the job almost before he sat down. He couldn't understand it, perhaps there was some catch and they had not been able to get anybody. It seemed unlikely, but on the other hand this was really a plum practice.

"Have you had many applicants?" asked Andy, puzzled by being accepted so easily.

"Seventy-three to be exact," said Stephen Hewitson, the senior of the two. "If you are puzzled why we have offered you the job so early, you will have to speak to my favourite nephew, a certain Dr David Hudson of St Daniel's Hospital, he said we could not do better than you. He does visit us from time to time, so if you do join us you will see something of him again."

"Good old David," said Andy.

"Of course," they said, "do bring your wife up to meet us and have a good look round before you decide."

Dr Shaw, the junior of the two, took him round to look at the surgery and at the empty flat upstairs which was usually used for putting up locums but would be available for Andy's use if he took the job. They also had a look around the little community hospital which had some geriatric beds, about eight midwifery beds and a casualty department. It all looked too good to be true.

Two weeks later he came up with Mary. Everybody liked each other on sight and the area, though not quite like Instow, was a very close second. There was a lovely little town, plenty of open country and the river. Both of the partners' wives, Mrs Hewitson and Mrs Shaw, were ex-nurses and of course had known each other for years and made Andy and Mary most welcome.

On the way back on the train Andy said, "Aren't we lucky."

Mary kissed him on the nose. "They're lucky to get you," she said.

"Rubbish," said Andy, "you're just prejudiced. All we have to do now is to get through my driving test."

"Hmm," said Mary, "there is also the small matter of my finals."

"Oh, I'm so sorry love," said Andy, "I'm being selfish, I'm sure you'll pass."

They snuggled up together and dozed for the long journey back to Devon.

Andy did pass his driving test but had become increasingly worried about Mary. Her exams seemed to have got to her. She looked pale, and wasn't eating much.

"Please don't worry," said Andy, "we have a good future all fixed. It would be lovely if you got your exams, but it isn't life and death." Andy had not seen Mary behave like this before. He thought he was the main worrier of the two.

The exams arrived and Mary was physically sick before both the two written papers. She really did not look well. Then the final day, the viva voce. Mary was sick in the morning again.

Andy had never realized that Mary had such a capacity for worrying. The examinations were being held in the teaching block. Andy wandered up to Fortescue Ward for tea and sympathy with Sister Sweet.

"God," said Andy, "I'll be glad when these exams are over. It will at least stop Mary being sick in the mornings."

"I doubt it," said Sister Sweet.

"What do you mean," said Andy. "How long do you think she will continue to be sick for?"

"Oh, about six to eight weeks," said Sister Sweet.

"Six to eight weeks," said Andy, puzzled, "she gets the results next week."

"Oh, she'll walk through the exam," said Sister Sweet, "she'll probably get the Gold Medal."

"But why do you say she'll continue to be sick," said Andy.

Sister Sweet smiled, "I don't know," she said, "they did say that you were the best Obstetric SHO they'd had for years, now I'm beginning to doubt it."

"What's that got to do with it," said Andy. Then suddenly he shot up and shouted, "My God, of course, she's pregnant, I'm going to be a Dad." He stood up and embraced Sister Sweet, picked her up and swung her around in a circle.

"Put me down," said Sister Sweet, "the patients will talk."

Andy waited in the flat till Mary came back from her exams. "Go and lie on the settee love," he said, "and I'll make a cup of tea."

Mary lay back pale and exhausted. Andy brought in a tray with a pot of tea, cups and some dry biscuits which was about all Mary was eating nowadays.

"Now tell me, mummy," he said, "when are we expecting little Mary to arrive?"

"You've guessed my secret," said Mary, "I didn't want you to worry, you would have stopped me taking my exams and wrapped me in cotton wool, and it's not going to be little Mary, it's going to be little Andy."

"Did everybody know except me?" asked Andy.

"Only Sister Sweet," said Mary.

"Gosh, I was so dumb," said Andy, "I would have diagnosed it in anyone else except my wife. You'll have to find yourself a new doctor."

"No chance," said Mary, "I'm sticking to you."

* * *

Mary did get the Gold Medal in her nursing exams and six months after they moved to the Thames Valley she was safely delivered of twins by Dr Hewitson in the little midwifery unit at Kangerford Hospital — a boy and a girl.